OH GOD, GOD, THE SUN GOES

DAVID CONNOR

A NOVEL

MELVILLE HOUSE
BROOKLYN, NY / LONDON

OH GOD, THE SUN GOES

First published in 2023 by Melville House
Copyright © 2022 by David Connor
All rights reserved
First Melville House Printing: June 2023

Melville House Publishing
46 John Street
Brooklyn, NY 11201

and

Melville House UK
Suite 2000
16/18 Woodford Road
London E7 0HA

mhpbooks.com
@melvillehouse

ISBN: 978-1-68589-062-9
ISBN: 978-1-68589-063-6 (eBook)

Library of Congress Control Number:
2023935081

Designed by Beste M. Doğan

Dance choreography by Laura Jeffery

Printed in the United States of America
10 9 8 7 6 5 4 3 2 1

A catalog record for this book is available
from the Library of Congress

For M

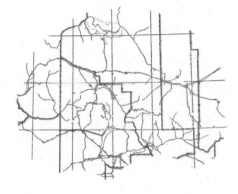

"Something is not the same / Something is different"
—LARAAJI

IT'S AS SIMPLE as it goes, the sun is missing. It's missing. It's missing. Been gone a month last someone's seen it.

There's a spot in the sky where it should be, a hollowed out circle that's sort of grey, like the absence of light—not darkness, different sort of absence—in a way, it's brighter than if the sun were there, more blinding even. Blinding grey absence in the sky.

Hard to see anything now, is what I'm saying, but still people are making do best they can. People are still moving along with their lives, going to work, going to school, cutting their nails, doing the laundry. It's only been a month.

Take Tom and Pete for instance. The two of them are sitting at a diner eating eggs. That's what they do each morning, same routine. I know this because I've been going to the diner each morning too, ever since the sun went missing, I've been eating eggs.

Usually I sit alone at a booth and watch Tom and Pete at the counter, talking about cars and roads and going. They say things about gasoline, about a woman they both know—I watch them as their yolks run down their plates.

Tempe, Arizona. Tempe. Tempe. That's where I moved when the sun went missing, about a month ago—moved because I thought maybe I'd find the sun in Tempe, or I'd find someone who could point me in the right direction. For some reason I thought Tempe when the sun went missing.

If the sun were underwater, I'd get a worm and fish it out.

If the sun went in a cave, I'd grab a flashlight and go searching. If the sun went to bed, somehow tucked itself under the covers and went to sleep, I'd find my way into its dream and say wake up, wake up. But none of these seem to be the case—for some reason, I thought Tempe, so I moved to Arizona.

I'm staring down at two eggs now, two eggs on my plate staring back up. There's a way that eggs stare that's more like looking, looking not staring, like the difference between seeing and eying. My eggs can't see me, is what I'm saying, of course they can't—they're eggs, I'm joking, okay okay, the waitress comes over and refills my glass.

Today, I've got a meeting with a Dr. H.A. Higley. I read an article about Dr. Higley in the newspaper that said he knew where the sun was, or at least that he'd been studying its movement for the past forty years. I found his number in a phone book and gave him a call because I figured he might know where to point me.

In the corner of the diner, Tom and Pete are still digging into their eggs. One of them makes a joke and the other slaps his knee like a cartoon stooge. In the other corner, there's a jukebox and Tom goes over to play a song on it. He shouts something to Pete and slips in a coin.

Wonder this time where she's gone . . .

"Jesus Christ," shouts Pete, putting down his fork. The

eggs on his plate start running, and Tom comes over with a big smile like a kid who's made a stupid joke.

Wonder if she's gone to stay . . .

"Come on," says Tom, reaching for Pete's hands. Pete pulls away and Tom laughs a little. "Pete, give me your hands," he says.

Ain't no sunshine when she's gone . . .
And this house just ain't no home . . .
Anytime she goes away . . .

"Withers?" says Pete.
"Why not?" says Tom. "It's a good song."

Tom starts dancing and motions for Pete to follow. Pete's face signals red as a *no*, as a stop sign—the lines in the diner bend a little as Tom dances around them, as Tom seems almost to change the space as he moves through it—like a painter, Pete looks on.

"Come on, Pete," says Tom. "Dance with me."

Pete signals no again. I look down at my plate and notice my eggs are gone—when I look up, Tom and Pete are dancing.

And I know, I know, I know, I know

Tom twirls Pete and the two of them dip and slide towards the counter. There's no making sense of it, it's simply happening—Tom and Pete are dancing in the middle of the diner, eight in the morning, it's a sight to see.

I know, I know, I know, I know, I know

Tom lifts Pete up a bit and the two of them start laughing like a pair of feverish drunks. Pete falls over in tears and in time Tom goes back to the jukebox to pick another song.

I know, I know, I know, I know, I know

Tom slips some quarters into the box and presses a few buttons but nothing happens for a little bit and Tom seems to get agitated. He puts in a few more coins and mumbles a word or two to himself.

I know, I know

"No! No! Goddamn it," shouts Tom, kicking the side of the box.

I know, I know

"Goddamn it," says Tom, face turning red like a tomato.

I know, I know

"Took my fucking money."

I know, I know

"Machine took my fucking money!"

I know, I know

"Goddamn!"

I know

"Goddamn."

I know

I get up from my seat and put a few bills down on the table as tip. Pete's started back at the eggs on the counter and Tom's still going on about his quarters in the jukebox. Goddamn, he mumbles, *goddamn*. I figure this is a fine time to leave the diner and head outside into the parking lot, and so I do and head into the heat of Tempe, Arizona, a heat of roads and cars and going. My car is on the other side of the parking lot, a baby blue toyota parked under the piecemeal cover of a Joshua tree and Santa Cruz, full tank of gas, a hundred thousand miles to its name.

If the car could speak, it would say *get in*.

I.

TEMPE, ARIZONA

THE WALK ACROSS the parking lot is a long one. It stretches out like a walk through a desert—a second becomes a minute and then an hour and then a second again. And after a few moments pass, a car pulls up next to me and someone rolls down the window.

"Hi there," says a woman, smoking a camel out the driver's side. She taps it against the window.

○

"You left this in the diner," she says, reaching down and grabbing an envelope—she hands it to me.

Ah, I mutter. "Can't believe I forgot."

She nods. A car pulls into the lot.

"Are you from Tempe?"

"No," I say. "I've been here a month."

"A month," says the woman, taking a smoke of the cigarette. Her hair is the color of the camel. "What brings you here?"

"The sun," I say. "I'm looking for it."

"I see," says the woman, staring now. "Looking for it."

"I am," I say.

The woman pauses for a minute, then speaks again.

"You know, my son, he's the star of the swim team at school."

○

"The day the sun went missing, he woke up and forgot how to swim. I swear to god, the day the sun went away, my son jumped in the pool and sunk straight to the bottom, completely forgot how to move his arms and legs, his teammates had to pull him out."

○

"He was going to swim at nationals. He'd been training all year."

"I'm sorry to hear that," I say, and the woman nods in agreement, blinking an eye.

"Anyway," she says, outing her cigarette on the side of the car. "I should get going," and within a minute, she taps on the gas and pulls suddenly away.

And for a moment I'm thinking about the bottom of pools, about the star of the swim team sinking to the bottom, waking up one morning and forgetting how to swim. The same day the sun goes missing, how odd.

Odd.
Odd.

A moment later, and I'm on the highway.

I'm on a road headed out of Tempe, towards the desert, winding and unwinding into the distance like a shoelace loosening itself—a burlap ribbon coming undone—Tempe is behind now, and the desert is ahead.

The desert is a long expanse of dirt, and rocks and crags and cacti that line the road like hitchhikers looking for a ride. The sky here is the same sky as anywhere, but brighter now, but somehow harder to see. As the desert goes on, its shapes come only slightly into focus, each rock a hidden object in sand.

Somewhere in the distance is a town named Sun City, which is where I'm headed today, to meet Dr. Higley. Sun City—of all names for a town in Arizona—is where Dr.

Higley lives, where he's lived for the past eighteen years with his wife, Martha Adie. Dr. Higley is now retired, but apparently in his day he was a leading mind in the field of solar astronomy, specifically helioseismology, the study of the sun and its seismic movements. Sun City is about forty miles away from Tempe, just north of Phoenix, and I should get there with plenty of daytime to kill.

The road I'm on now is becoming more and more narrow, which is nice because there's less to focus on—the mind can wander elsewhere, like towards the landscape and the thoughts layered in it—a thought of a rock passes beside me, and without knowing, I'm thinking about a mountain I once climbed—I'm thinking about the top of the mountain, how quiet it was, how you could see for miles in every direction— I'm thinking about how the mountain looked out over a desert, and how the desert looked very much like this one, sparse and wide open, with craters and crags everywhere.

A thought of a shrub passes by, and then a ditch, and a burrow, and suddenly the image of sand comes over my mind and I'm thinking about something someone once told me about sand. They said sand is like the past—it's the same and different each time you see it. They mentioned something about a footprint, about how things are always a little different, I forget exactly what they said.

I think about something else, and then another, and then I look down at the passenger's seat and notice the envelope resting there, the one the woman handed me outside the diner. It's blank and facing down, so I turn it over and notice a name printed on the front in black ink. I stare down at the letters but they're smudged and hard to decipher. I pull the envelope closer to my face, but the words are too jumbled to make out.

I focus on the road, then back on the envelope, and squint my eyes to see what it reads, but again, the letters spell out nothing. If I didn't know better, I'd say the letters weren't letters but pictographs—one of a mountain—one of a moon—one of a smaller mountain—another of a key.

I look out the window and notice a cloud float by—it's also unsure of its shape, floating east towards a plateau in the distance. I watch it morph from one thing into another, until I look down again at the envelope and notice a word beginning to form from the smudge.

From.
From, it reads.
Who? I think, and then I see it. In the distance, a cloud is turning grey.
M, it reads. *From M.*

The letter M

and suddenly I begin to cry.

And soon outside the window, the cloud begins to rain. It's pouring over a plateau in the distance.

From M, I say aloud, and mutter it again, until I realize I'm not sure who *M* is, and I'm not sure why I'm crying. *From M*, I say again, and realize the tears keep falling, there's no stopping them. I open the letter and read what's written, it's a single phrase:

Miss you, always

—M

M, I repeat to myself, and fold the note over. I place it back in the envelope and fold the envelope over, and over twice more. *Who's M?* I think, searching my mind as if searching the desert for a footprint but nothing, but nothing—after some time, I give it a rest and focus back on the road. I glue my eyes to the road signs and wait for something to signal the approach of Sun City, until I see it in the distance, a sign and then a town behind it. A desert town. A mirage rising from the ground.

I step on the gas and send the car flying. Outside the windows, the clouds have cleared—the sky is the color of a clue.

II.

SUN CITY,
ARIZONA

A CITY EMERGES from flatness. Like floating, like
falling slowly asleep.

If the town of Sun City appeared as a vision in a dream,
it would most likely be a daydream, and it would most likely
be a town where all the houses are the same more or less—the
lawns the same hue of green, the streets aligned in the same
way in each corner of the grid. At one end of town, there
would be a golf course with a large water fountain at the center, a man-made lake with ducks and lily pads and reeds along
the side. At the center of town, there would be a post office,
and a post office employee standing outside the office waving. In the corner of his eye, there would be a reflection of a
bird traveling at a few hundred feet aboveground, the bird's

vision taking in an aerial view of the scene, which reveals a town in the shape of a perfect O, a circle of houses surrounding a radial center and expanding out towards the desert in perfect symmetry. A Sun City, indeed, a town in the shape of a sun. If Sun City appeared in a dream, it would be a dream induced by the heat of the desert, or induced in a state of delusion brought on from driving too many miles. If Sun City were a town in a dream, it would be a town that doesn't make sense in the desert, too round, too green. If Sun City were a town in a dream, it would be a retirement town and all of its residents would be over the age of sixty-five. They would drive golf carts and wear similar shirts and make jokes whose punch lines ended with immediate laughter. The laughter would start violently and then trail off as everyone caught their breath. If Sun City were a town in a dream, it would be a desert town, a sleeping eye, a flattened sun. But Sun City is not a town in a dream but a town in Arizona, in the northern bounds of the Maricopa County line, just twenty miles north of Phoenix, a few miles farther from Tempe.

"Is everything all right?" a voice asks as I step out of my car into the asphalt parking lot.

A man stands at the center of the asphalt, a pair of binoculars in his hands. He's an older man, a resident of Sun City.

"Is everything all right?" he asks again, setting the binoculars to his side. The man is heavyset, blue-eyed, reddish face. On his shirt, he has a tag that reads *Parking Lot Attendant*.

"I'm all right," I say, gathering to my feet. "Just here to meet somebody."

"Who's that?" says the man, stepping closer.

"I'm looking for the sun," I say. "I'm here to see Dr. Higley."

It becomes clear that the man is a longtime resident of Sun City, a volunteer at the Visitor's Center. He pauses for a minute, and his face becomes redder.

"Higley?" says the man. "Higley."

"That's right," I say. "I believe he lives here."

"Well, this is a retirement town," says the man, looking straight at me then blinking. "We've got over twenty thousand residents here."

I look around.

"Higley," repeats the man, adjusting the tag on his shirt— it's a collared shirt, color of mud, he ruffles it. "You know what?" he says. "That name sounds familiar. Let me run inside and check."

The man turns around and disappears through a pair of double doors—Visitor's Center—a moment later, he comes back with a note in his hand.

"I got ahold of his wife," he says, "Martha," slipping me the note: "14073 Oakmont Drive, that's the address. And so you know, they're not expecting you for a few hours."

"That's what I thought," I say. "Thank you."

"If you've got time," adds the man in a low voice. "There's somewhere in town I think you should visit. It's not far from their house, good place to pass an hour."

"Sure," I say.

"It's the Sun City Museum," says the man. "Good place to pass time."

"Okay," I say. "I'll think about it"—and thank him.

"Just to pass time," says the man, smiling.

I nod and head back towards my car. And the man returns to his post and reaches for his binoculars. He waves as I leave the parking lot.

"Just to pass time," he yells again, waving. A minute later, he's gone.

A minute later, I'm driving through the middle of Sun City, past one-story bungalow houses, and rooftop satellite dishes, and sprinklers in yards twisting in precise mechanical spasms, relieving the grass of its dryness and heat. Must be the hour for that, because the sprinklers are moving at a fairly quick pace, turning each yard into a color of green that doesn't belong in the desert.

After some driving, a yard appears up ahead with a sign in the front reading *Sun City Museum*, so I pull over the car and step outside.

> Sun City Township, established 1960, Del E. Webb Construction Company.

A placard reads:

> Sun City Museum. Municipal Landmark.

The museum is a house at the end of the block, no different from the others around it—yard, rooftop, antenna—an identical antenna atop each slated roof, atop each one-story home in Sun City, pointing upward and awkwardly at the same desert sky. After a sprinkler's twist, I open the front door of the museum and step inside a dark room.

The only discernible trace at first is a smell, an odor like metal or perfume. As the door opens further the odor fades, and a room comes into focus, a living room set as if from the year 1960.

At the center of the room is a long oak coffee table—next to it, a couch and a sand-colored carpet stretching halfway across the floor. The couch is wrapped in a thin plastic slip-cover, and resting atop the table are a few items like a pennwood clock, a triangle ashtray, and a small silver tin of assorted caramel candies. From a room in the back, the sound of a radio can be heard just barely, playing an old-fashioned group like the Fleetwoods or the Everly Brothers.

Dreeeeeeeam dream dream dream

The sound of a person can be heard as well, shuffling some papers in a back office, until it becomes clear that they've noticed my presence, and the radio shuts off, a pair of feet scurrying out to the entrance room to greet me.

"Hi there!" a woman says, appearing from the hallway.

I say hi as well and the woman nods accordingly. A bright shade of eye shadow marks the upper half of her eyelids, and approaching closer, I can tell that the smell of the museum is coming from her.

"Hi," I say again, and explain who I am. The woman says I better make myself at home, and she closes the door behind us, as a light bulb sputters on in the corner.

What's striking about the house is how well it resembles a slightly older home—the woman explains that the furniture is preserved from when the house first opened. "It hasn't changed since 1960," she says. She mentions that it was the very first house constructed in Sun City.

I step farther in and the woman shows me a figure on the wall. It's a cardboard cutout of Del Webb, the town's founder. "*The greatest of all my accomplishments were the Sun Cities,*" it reads in bold lettering on a text square above him. He's not a handsome man, but maybe presidential in appearance.

"He's beloved around here, he really is," says the woman, beaming. "Everything in Sun City can be traced back to Del Webb."
"Seems important," I say.
"He was," says the woman, beaming. "Important."

The woman looks at me brightly, then retreats to the corner to fix the faltering light bulb.

"Del Webb," she mutters. "Remember that name."

I smile and step inside, and the woman returns to the back. Across the room, I notice a map on the wall with a layout of Sun City on it—a town indeed shaped after its namesake. If the map shows anything, it shows a town that was meticulously planned, a circular grid expanding out towards the desert in reticular fashion—emanating from a singular point in the middle which, according to the map, appears to be a parking lot, an empty spot, the lot I'd parked in earlier.

SUN CITY is a master-planned retirement community, reads the placard to its right. Developed by DELBERT WEBB and the DEL WEBB CONSTRUCTION COMPANY: to serve as an active-living retirement town for those in the latter portion of their lives.

Below: It is one of several across the United States. There are over a dozen Sun Cities built throughout the region alone. California, Utah, Nevada, Oklahoma, Kansas, Texas . . .

I turn around and notice the woman standing there.

"Isn't it great?" she says, hovering like a statue.

I nod and the two of us stare.

"It's just so nice," she says, smiling.

I say it sure seems that way.

The woman takes a loud, thrilled breath. "It's just *so* nice," she says, nearly shouting.

I hear a second sound coming from the back room and notice there's another person in the house. A moment later, a pair of feet shuffle out into the living room and a man appears, the woman's husband. "Berta!" he yells. Then he sees me and changes his expression a bit.

"Berta," he says, shifting tone. "Did you show our visitor the Del Webb room?"
"Yes, honey, I did, he knows."

The man stares at me and smiles affirmatively. A stern smile. "That's so good to hear," he says, assured. He stares at me until Berta speaks up.

"I just love everything," she says, beaming. "It's all so great."
"Everything in Sun City?" I ask, staring at Berta.
"Everything, honey. I love everything."

She points me to the corner.

DEL WEBB is an avid golfer and a part owner of the NEW YORK YANKEES franchise. He has played several rounds of golf with famous personality Bob Hope. Picture below.

"What do you think of it?" asks Berta's husband now, stepping in.

"Seems all right," I mutter, briefly looking around.

"You know Mr. Webb is beloved around here," he says, staring towards me. "Mr. Webb. Mr. Webb. He was a very special man, indeed, very special. A man. Special. Very special."

○

"Some would call him a *visionary*."

The man walks towards me. He appears somewhat sturdy and tall, as though he played a ball sport when he was younger. I look at his eyes and notice them soften slightly, as though he's taking something in.

"You look tired," he says to me, and I pause. "Like you've been traveling for a while." A second pause. I say it's true, I've been on the move now for a little bit, and the man says nothing, letting a certain type of quiet enter the room between us, the type that can only enter a room between breaks in a conversation. "You remind me of my brother," he says, smiling. "He was just like you, my brother, always traveling, always on the move."

I say nothing but let the man know I've heard.

"We used to joke, about my brother, we'd say he was always traveling, even when he was standing still. We'd say he was always half in a room, and half somewhere else. You don't need a car to travel, there's other ways," says the man, and I say I suppose that's true.

It's strange hearing the man say what he thinks of me, his impression, in a sense because I haven't had much time to think myself the past few weeks, driving around and around in the desert—it's not a landscape that lends itself to many mirrors. And on top of that, and more significant maybe, is that my mind's been kind of fuzzy the past month—since the sun went missing, I've sort of forgotten most things.

For instance, past a month, I don't remember much of the sun. What it looked like, how it felt to be underneath it, that round glowing orb—I mean I know what I'm looking for, but for some reason, I can't really remember its image. When I close my eyes, it's not there.

Better that way, I figure, because I imagine if I did remember the sun, it'd be too horribly sad, to remember something so big, that's missing now. In a way I think maybe I hit the road to forget it—when the sun went missing, I wanted time to keep moving forward.

Only consequence of course is that I've forgotten quite a bit, nearly everything really, since the sun's disappearance— all I can remember is the past month. Who I am, my whereabouts, that's all a mystery.

"Honey."

A noise clangs in the corner of the room and I look over. Berta and her husband are standing there, next to the lamp, which has just sputtered on. The two of them are staring at each other with loving eyes, pleased with their handiwork.

In the other corner of the room, I look at the clock, which has turned its hour hand a few notches down, *later than I thought*, I think, and realize already a few hours have passed. I turn back to Berta and her husband, who've begun remounting the lampshade over the bulb.

"I should go," I say in a soft tone and point to the clock. Berta and her husband notice and agree it's gotten late and tell me I should come again soon, and I say I'm sure I will, and they say they're sure as well.

"Sun City's not the sort of place you only come to once," says the man to me, and I nod as if I know what he's saying. "Too much to see," he says.

"I'm sure," I say. "I will."

"We'll be here," says Berta.

I look at the man and notice something change—his face shifts a bit. For a second I swear he looks exactly like someone else   like a ghost, or maybe Del Webb—but an instant later, the look goes away. I start to say something but can't think of any words.

"Remember that name," says Berta. "D-E-L E W-E-B-B."

"I will," I say, and Berta and her husband help me to the door. And before I know it, I'm inside Dr. Higley's house.

SKY,
AN INTERLUDE

A METAL OBJECT moves through a cloud, emerges on the other side in the shape of a plane. Its bright metal surface reflecting the bright grey color of the sky around it, and of the spot where the sun used to be, now hollow and gone.

> *Did the sun swallow itself?*
> *Or did the sky fold in two*
>   *and the sun fall in between?*

Whatever sky remains now is more blinding than before. And instead of darkness, a grey shell expands evenly across the earth and turns the ground below an altered color. Nobody can see the way they used to. Light doesn't carry across space like it once did, and still, it's hard to say exactly what's changed.

No memory comes readily to me now. If I try hard, I can glimpse barely into that old world once lighter. I can imagine who I might have been there, a person who held a job, a lawyer, a salesman selling insurance over the phone?

But no, the only questions I have lead to more questions. Like how it is this world is otherwise almost exactly the same. How it seems that life carries on in Sun City just as it always would, how the sprinklers move in the same mechanical fits, the cars turning along the same paved roads, life continuing as always.

On a lawn, a bird pecks its beak against the spigot of a sprinkler, draws no water, and flitters away. Outside a home, Martha Adie answers the door, and we walk inside into her living room, into a space that resembles the museum's almost exactly. I sit down on a plastic slipcover and Martha Adie begins speaking.

III.
SUN CITY, ARIZONA

"EVERY NIGHT, MY husband falls asleep with an egg
balanced on his forehead. He sleeps on his back and positions
himself so that the egg won't fall during the night. He sleeps
on his spine and never turns. He says it helps prepare him for
the coming day."

○

"He says the position of facing outward, with his back to the
mattress and the egg balanced on his head, prepares him to
face the coming day with an outward and balanced approach.
For many years, as an adolescent, H.A. would sleep on his
stomach. He would turn onto his chest and sleep with his face
pressed into the pillow, and this form of sleeping prepared

him very poorly. He said he wasn't sure why his body had chosen to sleep in this manner, but that at one point in his life, he concluded he would make the decision to turn around in bed and sleep facing out. He was a PhD candidate at the University of Phoenix in the Astrophysics Department at this point. He said it was during his first year of classes that he'd decided to make the change. He'd decided to face outward in sleep instead of inward. He said it was a *conscious decision*. That he forced himself each night to sleep on his back until it became natural. Until he didn't know any other way to sleep."

◯

"The egg came later. The egg came when Dr. Higley was the chair of his department. He was working on a difficult research assignment with several colleagues, something having to do with the seismic movement of sun waves. My husband began to sleep every night with an egg balanced on his forehead, because he thought it would prepare him for the day ahead. Each night, he would sleep with an egg balanced above his temples, and in the morning, he'd crack it open and eat it. He said it was helping him think."

◯

"He was troubled as an adolescent, my husband. He was always very intelligent, but he was never able to apply that intelligence to anything. He says it wasn't until he started sleeping on his back that he began to do anything of significance. He said it wasn't until he faced outward that he was able to think at all."

○

"His research paper was published that year in a prestigious journal, and eventually he was awarded the Einstein Prize in astrochemical physics. He really is a special mind, my husband. He's very respected in his field."

○

"But it's horrible," says Martha Adie, staring at me blankly with two sharp eyes wired like darts. "It's horrible, what's happened."

I stare forward and ask Martha to say more. Her pupils widen and narrow as planets moving in orbit, Mars and Mars, I imagine—Martha's eyes as two desert planets.

"Say more," I say, and Martha looks at me. Her pupils widen again and the lighting in her home seems to adjust accordingly. The television set in the corner changes hue and now the room takes on a darker tone.

"Well," says Martha, clearing her throat. "A few months ago, my husband started noticing something."

○

"Each night, he would sleep with the egg on his head, and each morning he would crack it open and fry it. He'd fry it in the pan and eat it for breakfast. A few months ago, my husband started to notice something change with the eggs. At first, it was a red dot. Just a small red dot he noticed in one egg. He cracked it and ate it anyway. Then he noticed the dot getting larger and larger, until the yolk itself was practically red. He didn't know what it meant, so he continued to eat the eggs, even though each morning, he noticed the dot was getting larger. The night before the sun disappeared, my husband slept for twelve hours, and when he awoke, he cracked the egg in the pan, and nothing was there. There was no egg inside the shell. It was completely empty. He hadn't even noticed the sun was gone at this point. He cracked the egg and saw nothing, then looked out the window, and realized the sun had disappeared."

How horrible, I mutter.

"It was," says Martha, with a serious glance. "It was shocking."

Martha looks away towards the window, as if recalling something.

"What did he do?" I ask, and Martha turns back to me.

"That's just it," she says, staring. "That's just it. He went into the refrigerator and grabbed another egg."

○

"Mind you, this is eight in the morning. He went to the refrigerator and grabbed an egg, then marched right back into the bedroom and fell asleep. He fell asleep on his back with the new egg resting above him between the temples. The same spot he'd always put it. Let me show you something," says Martha.

The two of us enter a hallway headed to a small room in the back of the house—the bedroom, and Martha pushes open a pair of doors to show me her husband lying asleep on their mattress. He's lying flat on his back, and sure enough, the egg is resting there directly atop his head. Nothing moves besides a slight breath, and some liquid in a bag of intravenous beside him.

"Dr. Higley," I mutter, and Martha nods quietly. She traces the floor with her gaze, glancing up only briefly to see her husband asleep in their bed.

"He's been sleeping there ever since the sun disappeared," says Martha. "The moment the sun went away, my husband came in here and fell fast asleep. He hasn't gotten up once."

I stare at Dr. Higley and notice his breath slowly raise and lower the down filling of their comforter.

"I had a doctor come see him. I had several doctors come see him. They all said the same thing. That he was sleeping. That he was in a very, very deep form of sleep. Lying supine, with the egg resting above his head."

"He must be thinking something over," I mutter, and Martha pauses very quietly.

She stares my way, and neither of us says anything for a while. "Something must be germinating in there," I mutter again, and Martha yields no response.

Instead she goes into the corner of the room and begins digging through a drawer, pulls out a sheet of paper and hands it to me. Her eyes narrow as she unfolds it, and I notice a tremor move up her finger slightly.

"This is the last thing he wrote before the sun disappeared," she says, turning the note open and handing it to me. The two of us look at Dr. Higley, who remains motionless in bed.

○

"It's the last note he left before the sun disappeared."

I stare down at the page and read it. At two words scribbled on the notebook paper.

Bumble Bee.

I squint down and reread it. "Bumble Bee," mutters Martha, pointing to the page. "That's the last note he left before the sun went missing. *Bumble Bee*."

I say nothing and squint down at the letters.

"He's pointing somewhere," says Martha, squinting with me.

Where? I mutter.

The two of us linger over the shape of the words, like smoke signals, like clues pointing in a given direction.

"You know, my husband and I met when we were fourteen years old. We went to the same high school together in Phoenix." Martha pauses for a minute and lingers over the sound of that word. "*Phoenix*," she says, "I miss that place," as a tremor moves up her finger again.

"You know, sometimes I think of Phoenix," she says. "And it makes me happy for a moment." Another tremor. "But sometimes I have nothing to think about," says Martha Adie, shutting her eyelids closed and launching into orbit. "And I feel so alone."

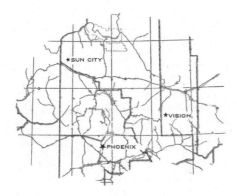

Theta wave moves below 3 Hz threshold. Subcortical
arrhythmic activity suggested. H.A. suspended in initial phase
of paradoxical sleep synchronization; normal cortisol levels;
norepinephrine release unremarkable.

IV.
BUMBLE BEE,
ARIZONA

IT'S AN HOUR'S drive to the tiny town of Bumble Bee.

The tiny twelve-person town of Bumble Bee, Arizona—a town caromed just west of the interstate 17 highway, which is a highway that cuts the state of Arizona directly in half, providing a north-south path between the two major poles of Phoenix and Flagstaff.

It's sort of strange here—the desert is an inverted sky, for miles and miles in each direction, the same sky, and the same desert road beneath it.

In these parts, the cacti have weird limbs. They have arms without hands—without palms. A sand shroud devils through the air and coughs up into the ground. Ahead, a dirt road meets the highway and veers off.

Some dead quiet. Another ten miles to Bumble Bee. A road like this is best traversed slowly, I realize—a busted wheel here could spell a long period of waiting. In the distance, a cow is lost grazing. A pack of them break off from the herd and head down towards the road. I hear some music coming in the distance.

> *Our guardian star lost all his glow*
> *The day that I lost you*

I notice one of the cows look towards my car, then back at the ground. I turn the radio to a station with better reception.

> *He lost all his glitter the day you said no*
> *And his silver turned to blue*

I tap the brake. The car slows down. A cow goes mooing in the distance.

> *Like him I am doubtful*
> *That your love is true*
> *But if you decide to call on me*
> *Ask for Mr. Blue*

I adjust the knob on my dash and correct the signal. The singer comes in quiet and clear. I turn the volume higher and roll down my windows.

The sky here is the same sky I saw in Tempe. It's the same sky I saw an hour ago in Sun City. The same colorless sky, the same bright high sky that looks so high and high away, the way the sky does after you've stared at the sun too long, except now the sun is gone, of course, and the sky is the same color in each corner of it.

In the upper-left bend, there's a half-moon waning in the final hours of dusk. It's a funny thing to look at the moon, especially now, with the sun gone missing. You have to wonder what light it's reflecting, and from where.

The moon is a joke, you think—it makes no sense. The radio crackles and corrects itself. The singer croons sweetly, like a chickadee flittering by.

> *I'm Mr. Blue, when you say you love me*
> *I'm Mr. Blue, when you say you're sorry*
> *Then turn around,*
> *heading for the lights of town*
> *Hurting me through and through*
> *Call me Mr. Blue*

I look to my side and notice a cow hunched by the road's edge. Its round boulder eyes buck out at me like question marks, like the lyrics to a song. I turn the radio a notch down and adjust the signal.

I stay at home at night
Right by the phone at night
But you never call
And I'll never hurt my pride
Call me Mr. . . .

The cow tucks its muzzle down and turns around. A waft of dung comes drifting in through the window like some melody through a pair of speakers—if the sun were out, it would be setting now, and the sky would be a golden ribbon of light. It would be a golden wound stretching above the desert, covering its blackened corners in an auburn glow.

There are many spots the sun could be hidden here. Many mounds of dirt yet unturned by hands, or shrubs unseen by peering eyes. If the sun were hiding, it would be hard to find it in the desert, with so much space to sift through, so much light hidden from the road.

As I look in my rearview, I notice some shrubs dancing along the side of it. Their stems turning left and right in the wind left by the wake of my car, like dancers waving their hands from side to side to signal something abstract in form. It's hard not to be nostalgic at an hour like this, not to imagine the shrubs moving as they had been.

Light is a deceptive thing, I think now. It's the sort of thing that can never really fix itself to time. Light seen now is different from light seen a decade ago, or a decade before that. Light seen as a child is not at all like the light that moves through the air now, not the same color or brightness. What accounts for this is probably hard to say, but I figure there's some explanation having to do with changes in the air, different densities of matter, different spectrums of light reaching earth. Still, none of this explains what we see today, with the sky as bright as it is, and the sun circled out of it completely.

I look up and notice a cloud again, puncturing its mark through the vanishing dusk. It vanishes too and leaves the sky alone, with nothing in it except bright fuzz, like an absent signal. The signal of the sky is an absent one, like a word with no clear meaning, like a word signifying nothing in particular, like a holy word to an unholy man who has no sense of meaning. *God. Holy.* Does a word with no meaning have only a sound? Is it only a note carrying over empty space? This is the color of the sky.

Soon the moon will rise higher and the sky will remain its same color, the way it has for a month now, bright as ever up above. Soon the town will appear in the distance, and I'll pull over the car to see if anything's there, if there are any traces of the sun in its midst, or clues to where it's been. I wonder if the sun is in this town, or if it's been here and left. I wonder if Dr. Higley's note will hold any substance. I step on the gas and watch the cows disappear in a cloud behind me. A shadow splits a dry bed in two, then covers the whole thing. The singer comes back in.

> *I won't tell you*
> *While you paint the town*
> *A bright red*
> *To turn it upside down*
> *I'm painting it too*
> *But I'm painting it blue*

Then I see it in the distance. Population twelve.

Call me Mr. Blue

A cow falls asleep.

Call me Mr. Blue

I adjust the knob.

Call me Mr. Blue

And soon the car rolls into Bumble Bee.

And a town appears.

And a town appears as large as a truck stop, with only a few houses and dilapidated wooden fences and a small structure in the back that looks like a makeshift apiary. The town is not necessarily what the term *town* usually applies to. This one has no main road, no fire station, no bank or convenience store. Instead the town is just a couple of houses, a few wheels parked in gravel pits, no different from the desert around it.

It's funny how *seen* a person might feel when there's nobody around them for miles. For miles, there's nothing and nobody and still I feel incredibly watched in this town, as if a pair of eyes were poking out from behind a screen door from one of the houses. There are only a few houses here and I see nobody in them. I wonder if they're sleeping in the late day, or gone somewhere else in their trucks. The whole town is as quiet as the ride over.

I step a few inches in and see the apiary more clearly now. It rises into the air with thin corrugated wooden slats, almost like an altar reaching towards the sky with an offering. Above it, I notice a small wooden pole pointed at forty-five degrees towards the air, an antenna of sorts, what looks to have been a sundial at one point, now catching no signal.

"Are you here to see the bees?" a voice calls from a yard away.

I turn around and see a woman standing there, a pair of eyes hidden in the shadow of her doorway. She doesn't seem to be a day above twenty, yet as I approach closer, I notice a thin string of silver hair streaking down the left side of her face.

"It's the bees," she says, peering through the screen door. "You're here to see the bees."

I pause and watch some wind kick dirt halfway across the town. It passes over my car like a reverse car wash, like a mile of driving. I step forward some more as the woman stays hidden in the shadow of her home.

I'm not sure, I mutter, and the woman looks at me skeptically. She keeps her eyes focused straight ahead, so I stop walking forward.

"I'm looking for the sun," I say, standing still, as the wind quits and the town is quiet again. "I've been looking for the sun."

As the woman stares at me, she becomes gradually disarmed, her face no longer guarded in scrutiny. *Ah*, she mutters, and disappears inside her home for a moment, returning a minute later.

"I have something to show you," she says, opening her door ajar, and I walk inside.

A hallway leads to a room in the back that's even more dimly lit, and along the walls are a series of images depicting bees in various locations. The entire house seems papered over in drawings of their likeness.

"I have hundreds of drawings of bumblebees in this house," says the woman, leading me further inside. "*This one is the drone bee*," she says, pointing to one drawing in particular. "The drones are large, passive male bees. They don't have stingers like the females. This one's a female," says the woman, pointing to the corner. "They can sting several times. I never go outside because of them," says the woman, looking at the drawing.

○

"I'm afraid of bees, to be honest with you. I'm obsessed with them. I know nearly everything there is to know about bees. But I would never go near one, no. I'm afraid of being stung, to tell you the truth. I'm afraid of being stung and then dropping dead, honestly. I know it's very unlikely, but I prefer not to risk it. I asked Hal, my cousin, to drill a hole into the hive next to this house, like a little peephole so I could see inside, so I could sketch the bees from my bedroom, and he drilled one for me about a year ago. Let me show you something," says the woman, leading me to a wall in the back whose plaster is drilled through the center. "Look," she says, and I peer through the wall to the other side, to a hive that appears in full prismatic display. Hexagonal units of beeswax resin, a golden nest of overlapping cells. Except as I look further, I can't manage to find the bees anywhere.

I can't see them, I mutter, and the woman turns from the wall. She stares at me with a worried expression overlying her face.

"That's just it," she says, staring. "When the sun disappeared from the sky, the bees had nowhere to go, of course. When the sun went missing a month ago, the bees went missing as well."

○

"Bees use the sun to know where they are. They have a special sort of photoreceptor on their eyes that detects the angle of the sun's rays. That gives them a coordinate understanding of space. People like us, we remember space as a series of images. *That sign there. That dirt road.* But bees remember space as a series of points. That's why they're so good at returning to the hive every day after pollinating. But that's also why they're missing now, and I'm not sure they're coming back."

The woman reaches up to the top of the wall and pulls a drawing down from it, laying it flat on a table before me. She points to the middle of it and gestures to a bee in the center. She circles it with her hand.

"It was the strangest thing," she says, looking down at the drawing and gesturing to the bee in the middle. "But the day before the sun went missing, a worker bee came into the hive and began shaking its stinger. It began doing this *waggle* dance, which I'd never seen a bumblebee do. Usually it's only honeybees that do that kind of dance. But the day before the sun went missing, a worker bee came into the hive and began shaking its stinger in dramatic fits, moving in a figure eight pattern. All of the bees were gathered around it. Even the queen bee seemed interested, she was watching. This dance went on for quite some time, hours even, and I was watching it in my room through the peephole, and I was trying to keep track of each movement as it was happening on this sheet of paper you see before me." The woman points down to the pad, gesturing towards a series of lines and arrows denoting the repetitive movement of the bee through space. "The dance went on for hours, the same sort of motion again and again, which to me meant the bee was signaling to a very distant location. That the bee must be pointing somewhere very far from the nest, a dozen miles or so. The dance went on for several hours, and judging by the position of the stinger and where it was pointed, I could determine where the bee was signaling to. Wherever the bee was signaling, I think the sun might be there. Wherever the bee was pointing its stinger, I think the sun is hidden."

The woman looks up from the page, her eyes circled with a ring of exhaustion, as though she's been staring at these drawings ever since the bees disappeared, as though somehow their arrangement holds a crucial wiring of sense.

"Wherever the bee was pointing, it's south of here. Coordinate three-three point four-four-eight by coordinate one-one-two point zero-seven-four. Remember, this is an estimate. Wherever the bees went, I believe it's this location."

The woman stares at me, waiting.

"Where is that?" I ask, and she pulls down a map from the

wall. She points to a spot and circles it with her index finger. "*Phoenix*," she says. "The sun is in Phoenix."

"Of course," I say. "That makes sense. *Phoenix*."

The woman nods soberly and looks up from the map.

"What was your name again?" I ask, looking at the woman now more clearly from across the room.

"Clara," she replies.

○

"Clara Morales."

"I see," I say to Clara. "It was nice to meet you."

Clara nods and looks up. She takes a moment to stare at me.

"What's your name?" she asks, curious now.

"I'm not sure," I say, and Clara looks at me strangely.

"Mr. Blue," I say. "I'm Mr. Blue."

"*Blue*," repeats Clara, without missing a beat, and the sky gleams bright. "Why are you here, Mr. Blue?"

"I'm not sure," I say. "I'm looking for the sun."

"Where are you from?" she asks.

Again, I say, "I don't know."

"My family has lived in Bumble Bee for three generations. And before that, we lived in Mexico. This used to be Mexico, you know, all of Arizona. The Sonoran Desert."

"You don't say," I mutter, looking at Clara. "It's a small town here, Bumble Bee."

"Very small," she says. "Twelve of us. Twelve people."

A cloud appears in the sky.

"I bet you can relax now," I say. "With the bees gone."

"That's true," says Clara, "I feel a lot calmer."

"But I bet you miss them," I say. "Of course."

"You have no idea," says Clara. "They were everything I had."

"I know," I say. "I'm sorry to hear that." And the two of us hug. I feel a teardrop fall but it's unclear from whom it fell. I feel something that ought to feel like closeness.

That night, I find a motel to nod off.

V.
TEMPE,
ARIZONA

In my dream, I'm in a diner in Tempe. A waitress comes over and asks what I'd like to eat, and I say two eggs, *fried*, and she says *how would you like them*? A thought. *Over medium*, I say, and after a moment, a plate appears with a pair of eggs in front of me.

I look across the booth and notice someone sitting at the other end of it—a woman whose hair is the color of cornmeal, the color of the windowpane that rests to our side, next to the booth.

I know her, I think. *M.*

I mutter, and she looks over, and I feel myself turn to glue, like an ache that carries itself through my bones and makes them molded and egglike. *I miss you*, I think, and I say it out loud, and *M* waits to respond in the way that an actor waits to respond in a certain sort of play that's not meant to represent reality. *Of course.*

M, I mutter, and again she looks over and I reach out to touch her hand, and I clasp it across the table and feel its warmth. It's the hand of someone who knows something, who holds a secret, and I tell her that.

I stare at her then. She stares. Her face is rosy and swelling like steam rising from a coffee mug. She stares at me and asks if I know about the sun and I say *yes*, that it's *missing*, and it's been missing for *a month*. She smiles and turns towards the window, gesturing for me to look with her, and then I see in the distance, a red sun hanging in the sky in the final hours of daylight. *The sun*, I mutter in my dream, and look over at *M*, who smiles again. I tell her that I would like to see her more clearly, if she could move the mug away, but she says *no, I'm sorry*, and her face remains clouded in steam. Her face remains a cloud.

Do you remember who I am? she asks plainly, and I say *yes, of course, you're M*, I say. *I've been missing you.* She nods and removes her hands from the table. I let go of my grip. *M*, I mutter, and realize *M* and I had been lovers, that *M* is someone I had loved. A waft of steam slips down her nose and makes her eye visible for a second, a button, then disappears before I can really see it. I feel something move under the table like a bear and realize it's myself. I feel hungry, I realize.

I tell *M* she should get something to eat but she says *no*, she has to *go* soon. I say *why*, and she says *she does*. She has somewhere *to go*. I say I've been going for so long, it's nice to be here, it's nice to sit. She says she *knows* but she can't *stay*. She has to *go*.

I say *for how long*, and she says *forever*, she doesn't know. *Maybe longer*. I laugh and say *you're joking*, and she smiles and says *no*, it's true. *It's true, I have to go*.

Then under the table, I feel the hunger again. I feel a movement shifting in my lap. I ask *M* if I can touch her now, and she says *no*, not here, there are people eating. *Please*, I say, *I'd like to touch you*, I'd like to be closer, and *M* says *no* again, softly, I want to see her through the steam, her face seems so nice I could die in it.

I don't remember exactly, but I think I ask her then if I could possibly touch myself, under the table, where no one would see, and she says *sure*, it's okay, as long as no one notices. So I undo my belt and feel a pang immediately, even in the dream, I know I shouldn't be doing this under the table. I look at *M* and feel myself become hungry some more.

There's a smell of course, like coffee and toast in the diner. And somehow these smells blend themselves together through *M*, I don't understand the physics of it. I miss it, I think, that smell, not like a smell in waking life, only a smell that could exist in dreams, the diner in Tempe doesn't smell like this does. I grab my cock and tug it, and imagine it under the table inside her. I imagine the grip of her wetness tightening softly around it and the steam from the table clearing so that I could see her in the open, so I could see her breasts and hold them firmly in my hands like a pair of mugs. As I picture this, the hunger grows.

I feel bad, I say, *I'm sorry*, and *M* smiles and says *it's okay*, and I say I'm sorry again and she says *it's okay, I love you*, and for a moment I feel my desire shift, like a hunger turning towards a lightness, like a hunger moving from a desperation to a tenderness, a sweetness I hadn't felt in a long time. A gulf thinning. I finish under the table and clean myself up, and apologize to *M*, who says it's okay, it's okay.

I have to go now, she says, and I say *okay* despite the hole in my chest. I watch her leave the table and exit through the back door, and outside the window, the sun is setting as well, and the sky becomes dark with night. At this moment, I wake up from the dream and realize I have a letter waiting in my drawer, addressed from *M*.

It reads as such:

The sun is not in a quilted blanket, or an oven left on high. It's not lurking in an old attic or a dark corridor still unsearched. It's not below the leaves of trees, or cooing in the soughs of wind. No, the sun is somewhere else entirely, not like any of these places. The sun couldn't be hidden in the ocean, or floating above a lake bed. It couldn't be at the base of a dune, or stuck above a rocky cliff. The sun is nowhere like this, nowhere you could stumble and find it. No, the sun is somewhere murkier, somewhere darker and damper and funnier. The sun is under a nose on a face with no features, that's where you'll find it. The sun, if you seek it, is under your nose, but your nose is made of broken glass. No, the sun is in the Mind, that's where it is, the Mind is the harbor of the sun, go there, and you'll find it. With love, forever, M.

I put the letter down and stand next to the bedside table. The letter reads as a riddle of codes, like *M* knows where the sun is, and she's leading me to it. Except the language is so hard to parse it's not clear exactly where she's pointing, though I imagine she knows something, about the sun, or perhaps she's with the sun, as she's writing it. I don't know really who *M* is still, though I feel a pang in my chest as I read it, like the pang of a love that was once so bright then gone.

VI.
PHOENIX,
ARIZONA

THE STREETS OF Phoenix are covered in soot and dust, and the slag from the metal of buildings rises into the air and dissipates slowly into fog. Phoenix is a city that asks you to forget it—it asks for nothing else.

On a street corner in the southern portion of the municipality, a bar flashes its dull neon sign into the thoroughfare of traffic. And everywhere, the city of Phoenix moves about with the same relentless pace, the cars moving in straight lines through the concentric grid of the city, where the streets cover themselves with more and more soot by day. I look down at a map in my hand and at a coordinate circled near the center, point 33.448, 112.074—Phoenix, Arizona—it reads. *I'm close,*

I think, and look up for a moment, and notice a sign blinking in sharp orange letters, *THE MIND*, it reads, and blinks, and reads again. *THE MIND* is the name of the bar, I figure—it blinks in neon letters against the grey backdrop of the brick facade.

Inside the bar, the lighting is so poor you can't see. The bar is just a dark room with a few red lights pointing towards the counter where a woman stares in a blue sweater serving yellow beers to men in jackets.

I walk over and order a yellow beer and sit down at the bar for a moment, until I notice a man at the other end of it with a pair of boots also drinking a yellow beer, and we strike up a conversation.

"Have you lived in Phoenix long?" I say to the man, and he nods as long as my question. *Long*, he draws out. *Lonnng*.

I think to ask something else but before I can, the man goes on telling me that he's lived in the south end of Phoenix for thirty years, and before that, he grew up just outside the city. "I'm a plumber," the man says, and then I notice his bag with the name of a plumbing company on it, *Plumbing Masters*. He winks at me and kicks the bag.

"Never seen you in here before," he says, and I say that's true because I've never been to Phoenix. I ask him if he comes to the bar often, but I realize how stock that sounds.

"I sure do," he says, and stares into his yellow mug. He swirls it and waits for the foam to settle. He's maybe fifty years, maybe more with good aging. "What are you doing here?" he asks in a direct tone.

"The sun," I say.

The man looks up from his mug and stares at me gingerly, softly. "Good for you," he says, and finishes a swig of foam.

"I think the sun might be in Phoenix," I say, and the man smiles in a tempered way.

"You've never been here before?" he asks, and I answer *no, I haven't*. "Never?" he repeats, and I look up without saying anything more.

"You know how Phoenix got its name?" he says to me in the tone of a setup with no punch line—I say *no* and the man takes a swig of his beer and pushes it to the side. He rests his hands on his lap, and his belt has a scorpion on it.

"Phoenix is the traditional land of the Hohokam people," he says, shifting his attention towards me. He pauses in a subtle way, in the sort of way that suggests a gathering of thoughts. "*Hohokam* is a word that means *those who have gone*," he says. "The land we're on now used to be their home."

I stare into my beer and watch it glisten—it seems to fill up with more beer the longer I stare. The man goes on with more details, leaning into his glass.

"The descendants of the Hohokam are the Tohono O'odham and the Akimel O'odham. The word *Hohokam* comes from their language. We don't know what the Hohokam called themselves."

I say *okay* and set my beer aside for a moment to listen some more. The lighting in the bar is brighter now, and the scorpion on the man's belt begins to move around, begins to dance in dark red and shadow. The man adjusts in his seat and goes on.

"The Hohokam were here for over a thousand years, and they irrigated the land with a canal system. I say this because when the white settlers came, after the civil war, they saw the canals and began to build over them. They built the city of Phoenix from the ruins of the Hohokam civilization." I say *I see* and nod. "That's why it's called Phoenix," says the man. "Because it was built from the ashes of a former civilization."

"Like the phoenix," I mutter, and the man nods in a sober way, as the two of us stare forward.

"My mother and her family live on the reservation south of here. They're Tohono O'odham."

I say something and nod again. There's a long pause where nothing is said, where the edges of words have time to absorb or not absorb into thought. Into the deep crevices of thought, the edges either absorb or pass along.

"You know what's funny about the sun?" says the man, changing the subject. "What's funny about the sun is that it has no edge. It's a sphere. There's no tracing the end of such a thing."

"What do you mean?" I say.

"I mean it's odd that something like that could go missing."

The man stares at me coolly and communicates something without a word, without anything. He hardly shifts in his position, and yet I find some form of language passed along. He turns back in his seat and orders another beer from the woman at the counter, who seems preoccupied with the television set overhanging the bar. The station is playing a program with cars on it, and the woman doesn't seem to care for much else.

I look over and notice the man's bag, *Plumbing Masters*, on the floor beside him. The cover of a book pokes out from the zipper, *Quantum Sun*, and below it, the name of the author appears in print, in familiar letters: *H.A. Higley.*

"Higley?" I say, looking over at the man who notices my attention. He looks down at his bag and sees the book there.

"That's right," he says, "*Quantum Sun.*"

The man reaches down to place the book on the counter.

"It's one of my favorites," he says, turning it towards me. "And I've read it about a hundred times."

I stare down at the book cover—the image of a sun

splayed in the bottom-right corner, beside it, Dr. Higley's name in bright font.

"There's a chapter in here called 'De-Centered Sun Hypothesis,' which is Dr. Higley's explanation of sun disappearance."

So he knew then? I mutter. "He knew this was possible?" And the man nods, turning the book open to a page in the back.

"Dr. Higley explains that the sun can go missing under certain conditions, and if those conditions are met, the sun can simply disappear from sight."

The man turns to another page.

"He explains it as a sort of metaphysical phenomenon. That the sun isn't really gone from the sky, but that its light can no longer be seen. That the sun is missing because of a rift in metaphysical space."

"What kind of rift?" I ask, and the man grabs his beer.

"The sun can disappear if something happens to *the Mind*. If something happens to *the Mind* that causes it to go awry, the sun can disappear from sight."

"Whose mind?" I ask, and the man stares at me for a long period of time, then turns and signals to the end of the counter for another beer.

"Any mind," he says under his breath. "The sun can go missing from any mind."

I look at the man and pause. He signals again to the end of the counter, then turns back to me.

"Something happened to metaphysical space, and now the sun is missing."

Finally some beer arrives, and the man rests his voice to watch it chute into his mug. He sees it rise up as a mountain might above a tectonic plate, creating a summit of foam which he brings to his lips and wears like a mustache.

"You know, in O'odham culture, there's a traditional myth known as the Man in the Maze—it's on our emblem, you see it depicted on our flag—there's a man and there's a maze, and at the center of the maze is the sun. Could be a man, could be a woman, doesn't matter. But this emblem is meant to represent a person's journey through life, all of their choices and decisions, their dreams and aspirations and hopes, and when they get to the center of the maze, they have an opportunity to look back on all of those decisions, and dreams, and wishes, before they're greeted by the sun god who welcomes them into the next world."

The man reaches in his pocket for a pen and draws the symbol on a paper napkin, then turns it towards me so I can see.

"For us, the sun has been missing for years."

He folds the napkin over into a ball and pockets it, then takes another swig of foam.

"The sun has been missing our whole lives," he says, finishing the glass.

A car passes through the television screen, and the woman pours a glass of yellow beer for herself and downs it. I turn towards the man and say I need to use the restroom, and he says *sure*, so I leave the counter for a moment and wander to the back of the bar where the lighting is even darker. It's even bleaker here, and I can hardly see an inch in front of me—I prod open a door and head down a long hallway that's even darker and harder to see—I prod another door and head in the wrong direction, then make a left and head into a hallway that seems to lead nowhere resembling the restroom. On the walls here are a series of placards all labeled with different names for the different rooms. *Medulla Oblongata*, one reads. *Substantia Nigra*. *Corpus Callosum*. *Odd*, I think, so I turn around again and leave the hall, then head into another, and another one, until finally I see a door at the end of a long stretch, a placard labeled *Caballeros*—so I go inside to relieve myself at a stall.

On the wall above the paper roll, I notice a note scribbled

in black sharpie ink, ill-shapen letters spelling out a bible verse. I squint and read as I undo my belt, and start going at the stall.

> *John 1:1   In the beginning was the Word, and the Word*
> *was with God, and the Word was God.*

I squint again and reread it. I read it the way one reads notes written on walls.

> *In the beginning was the Word, and the Word was with*
> *G-d, and the Word was G-d.*

God, I mutter, and realize all the *o*'s are missing from *God*—instead of *o*, it's *G-d* with a dash.

As I finish and zip my pants, I scan the verse a few more times—*with G-d, was G-d*—no *o*—*with G-d, was G-d*—then splash my hands with water and head back out.

In no time, I'm back in the bar and notice the man is gone from the counter, and yet his mug is still full of beer and foam. He's left a few bills down on the table as tip— besides that, everything else is the same in the bar. The woman is still in the corner drinking a beer, the lighting is still dark and red, and the music is still playing from the jukebox—a song whose lyrics are too ambient to distinguish from its chords.

In a moment, I leave the bar and head back out onto the streets, which are the same streets I came in through—except now somehow the streets seem slightly different. No doubt, they're the same—the same pavement, the same intersection, the same thoroughfare of traffic moving along—but something is off about it—the cars no longer move with an ordinary speed.

I stare back at the bar and notice that the sign itself has changed, that it no longer blinks with the same words—*THE MIND*—but something different.

Strange, I think, and look up, and see now that the name of the bar has changed from *THE MIND* to *PHOENIX*—the bar and the city have traded names.

I look down at the map in my hands, the same map as before, same streets and layout, everything identically the same, except the names of places on the map are different. At the top of the key, my eyes glide to the name of the city—*PHOENIX*—as it read before, but now even that name is new. As I stare down at the map, I watch it turn orange from the dead glow of dying neon above, from the dead glow of *PHOENIX*. But the map no longer reads *PHOENIX* on it, no. Instead, something else.

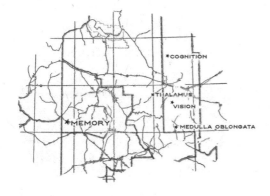

Cerebral hemispheres imaged using positron emission
tomography; ventricular system is midline and normal in size and
configuration; occlusions along various central nerve tracts in H.A.
suggest underlying psychogenic disruption.

VII.
MAP READS
THE MIND

OUTSIDE THE BAR, a city appears just as Phoenix—
no different in any particular way. The same roads and cars
and buildings stretching out towards the desert in incremen-
tal loops, a cosmopolis expanding within a desert of sand.

From the valley of the sun, a city rises just as Phoenix had,
yet as I look down at the map in my hands, I see that it's now
labeled *the Mind*.

Map reads *the Mind*.

What city is this? I wonder, but let that thought pass along,
like so many other thoughts that drift in and pass along without ever seeing daylight.

The dead glow of the bar sign turns the avenue orange. From outside PHOENIX, the city of *the Mind* appears as any city would, traffic leaving the desert and traffic entering. The same horn sounds, intersections, skids of wheels on pavement. And yet, each sound takes on a new cadence, a new buzzing just below the surface.

From midair, a bee appears and disappears into space. It flies by my ear and away again, forming a figure eight in the air until its noise becomes indistinguishable from the bar sign above, from the dead glow of dying neon.

Soon the entire city buzzes with a similar potential, with the sense of a riddle below its surface.

For whatever reason, I have the strange sense that I've been here before. Not to PHOENIX, but to *the Mind*. Its topography strikes me as no different from any city in Arizona. Even the names of neighborhoods, like the one I'm in now, *Medulla*, strike me as oddly familiar. *I've been here before*, I think, and yet I can't say whether I have.

A bee appears once more and flies away. Its noise and the noise of PHOENIX blend into an electric buzzing. Somewhere within this sound the sun is bound to be hidden. Beneath the surface of streets and boulevards, I sense a hidden passage waiting to unfold.

From the dust that surrounds it, *the Mind* stretches out towards the desert like dead matter forming and clumping into shapes, a system of nerves pulsing through channels of energy, sending distant signals from one end of the grid to another—from one end to another, the city buzzes with sense.

I head back towards my car and hit the gas, as the orange light of PHOENIX fades behind me, as the neighborhood of *Medulla* disappears into an afterthought. Neighborhood after neighborhood pass along the road, winding in knots towards the city center, which rises from the ground in familiar shapes, in the shapes of buildings rising from the ground and masking the streets in their shadow.

VIII.

AT THE HEART

OF *THE MIND*,

A TRAIN STATION

AFTER MILES OF driving, I pull over the car and park it at a meter along the side of the road. I put some quarters in a slot and give myself a few hours, enough time to walk around and see the neighborhood by foot.

Up ahead, a railway station emerges through the dust cloud of its own making, a grand central concourse at the heart of what must have been *downtown*. I step through its large wooden doors and walk inside, into a great domed hall with a grand clock in the back, its glass panel now sooted over by railway dust.

Through the pollution of sound coming from the high-speed rail lines, a storm of passengers exits a train and stammers its way to a distant gate. The noise of their feet plodding on the floor makes the vague sound of hail, of Phoenician rain.

Through their cloud, a conductor looks down at his watch outside a commuter train parked momentarily at its gate. I study his face and see it appear oddly familiar, like the face of someone I've recently met, a resident of Sun City, which now seems like a world away, and possibly is.

As the man stares up at me, I notice his face appear almost exactly as the man's outside the Visitor's Center, the same reddened visage as the attendant of the parking lot. However, now, as I stare closer, I notice that he appears slightly younger, an inch taller and without his binoculars.

"Can I help you?" he says, and I step back for a moment. I notice his voice is not as I'd remembered, not as low or distinct.

I can tell that the man must think I'm from a different planet. I don't look any different from the people here, nor they from me, but I feel now as if I've landed on some foreign land, some nonphysical space whose laws I don't fully comprehend.

"Are you looking for a train?" he says finally, noticing my confusion. For a moment, my focus trails off towards the end of the platform then back, wondering where exactly I am.

○

"This is *Thalamus Station*," he says, adding, "All rail traffic moving through *the Mind* moves through here."

A flood of passengers descends the platform as their train time is announced, mounting the locomotive as it quickly huffs off in a cloud of its own fume. The man looks up at the central clock, which signals a time I can't see through the sooted glass panel.

The entire railway station is hard to see, a thick layer of dust silted through the air and forgotten.

"My train leaves in a few minutes," he says, and I nod *okay*, but first ask where the man is headed, and he says along *the Corpus Callosum*, a rail line running through the center of the city.

"I see," I say, and imagine a high-speed rail running somewhere within the borders of the city resembling Phoenix, which is a city I've never really seen.

"I should mention," says the man. "Trains are running a little different now," he explains, warning that it's been this way for a month. "Trains aren't running their usual routes."

He pauses as a commuter rail shudders in place.

"Pathways have been interrupted."

The man's focus trails off again towards the end of the platform, then back over. A train pulls into its gate and another storm of passengers descends.

"All rail lines are rerouted," he says, adjusting his shirt now, which he ruffles.

I begin to wonder whether the sun isn't missing at the end of some errant rail line, some forgotten part of *the Mind* the train no longer goes. The conductor looks back at the clock, which signals a time I still can't see.

"This train heads *north*," he says, "If you want a ride. North of here is a neighborhood known as *Hippocampus*. The train doesn't stop there anymore, but if you get off near it, you can walk. Might reach it that way."

I think about my car parked at a meter but then forget. I forget and the car becomes an afterthought, an object fixed in a previous time, lost somewhere back there and not here. "One more thing," I say to the conductor, as the central clock makes a sound. *"Whose mind is this? Whose mind are we in?"* The engine of the train shudders in place and the conductor looks around. He quickly boards the locomotive and makes a call for passengers, so I find the nearest doors and step in. *Whose mind is this?* I mutter to myself, and find a seat by the window, sitting down to watch *the Mind* reveal itself in time.

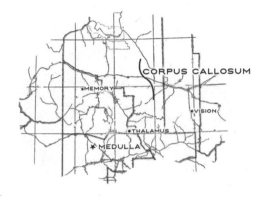

Subject presents amnesiac dissociation.
Occlusion along *Corpus Callosum* suggesting bifurcation
of left and right cerebral hemispheres.

IX.
A RAIL LINE
RUNS THROUGH
THE CENTER

IT SPLITS THE *Mind* in two as a mirror east and west.

The afferent cord, the one I'm on now, runs to the northernmost tip of the city, passing streets and neighborhoods along the way, stopping at each station to collect new passengers and let old ones off.

A man sits down across from me in the train car and opens a newspaper whose banner reads *The Phoenix Times*. He's an older man with stalky hands and mumbles to himself as he reads the front page. The train comes to a full stop at a station and a few passengers pour off. The platform sign reads *Caudate Nucleus*, which disappears quickly as the train rolls away.

I look at the man again, who's hidden mostly behind the tall pages of his newspaper. His hair pokes out in a thick silver coif that seems well maintained. Everything about the man, his comportment, his suit jacket, seems well maintained, as though a man weren't there but a cardboard cutout instead.

After some minutes, I notice him rummage through a brown leather briefcase, placing his newspaper inside and then pulling out a book. He folds it open on his lap and squints down at the pages.

Quantum Sun, I mutter, looking over at the book, then up at the man. He turns to me, surprised.

"That's right," he says, curious. "That's exactly right."

He folds the cover over for a moment and stares at me. His eyes suggest an unspoken familiarity, a sameness that seems both obvious and impossible.

"I'm Delbert Webb," he says, extending his hand, which I shake without thinking. "*Del E. Webb*," the man repeats, winking, as though handing me a business card.

"I know you," I say instantly, and Del smiles with recognition. "I know Sun City," I say. "I was just in Arizona."

"Arizona," says Del, beaming. "*The original.* My favorite of all the Sun Cities." He smiles again and scoots closer to me.

A conductor comes by to check tickets, so I pay for one—and he punches a hole in it.

The train rolls into a station, *Substantia Nigra*, and waits there for a moment.

"I've built over a hundred Sun Cities. Over two hundred," says Del. "But Sun City, Arizona remains my absolute favorite. It's like your first great love, you know," he says. "You never love anyone else exactly the same way." The doors to the station remain open, and a wind drafts in through the cabin. The neighborhood of *Substantia Nigra* is hard to see through the dust-blown wind, through the soot whirling by the platform.

"You don't own anything until you own real estate," says Del, noticing my attention drift for a moment. I turn back and nod unconsciously. Del's stare remains unwavering. "That's why I've always loved my line of work," he says, with an insinuating tone. "You don't own anything, until you own *space*."

I think for a moment and say nothing. Del goes on again without a beat, until the doors to the station close and the train keeps moving.

"Do you own *space*?" he asks me, and I think for a moment. I don't know how to answer and mutter *no*, explaining that I've been on the go now. I've been going for over a month and the only thing I have is my car, which I've parked back at the station.

"You don't own anything," repeats Del Webb, "until you own real estate."

He nods and another station passes outside the train window and disappears before I can see. Del turns back to his book and begins reading again, so I turn towards the window and watch *the Mind* morph slowly northward.

The Mind morphs as any city would. Streets alter and become wider, become more narrow and congested with traffic, with bumper-to-bumper, with standstill. The streets interweave like channels of nerves, like branches reaching to meet axonal stems—a hidden pulse is transmitted just below the surface of the streets, out of visible range. If squinting keenly, the appearance of the city alters even more, becomes less flat and more riddled with sulcus and gyrus formations, grooves in the earth bundling up and down like crags and craters between the crust. A pothole juts here and there, a crack in the pavement. And below, the deeper city can be sensed but only in a moment, only in a passing shadow.

At the next stop, a few passengers climb on and Del scoots

his briefcase closer to his knee, nudging me with it slightly on accident. "You know," he says, turning towards me. "I've always wanted to build a city on the surface of the sun." I pause and look at Del, whose eyes suggest utter seriousness— *on the sun*—his eyes expand wide-angle like lenses. "I've always wanted to build a Sun City on the surface of *the sun*," he repeats. "It's always been my greatest ambition." I mutter something and Del scoots closer, nudging me with his knee. "Picture it," he says, smiling with his teeth. "You look up at the sky, and there's a city there." I stare out the window and picture it, looking up at the bright sunless sky of *the Mind*.

I can't imagine it, I say, and Del nods. "Well, of course not," he says. "The sun is gone now"—gesturing down to the book, *Quantum Sun*. "You know this author, he's one of my residents," Del says, emphasizing the word *resident* with an undue weight. "He lives in Sun City, Arizona," says Del, "though I'm assuming you knew that already," and I nod.

○

"I'm going to tell you something," says Del, lowering his voice in a stage whisper. "Dr. Higley *knows* something," he says. "He *knows* something, and he's here in *the Mind*." The train corrects itself over a curve and shears the metal track, making a strident sound. "Dr. Higley knows about the sun," says Del, staring me directly between the eyes. "That's all I'm going to say."

The train makes a turn around a curve and straightens just as quickly. Just as quickly, the train moves down the middle of *the Mind*, splitting east and west in half. After a few station stops, Del gets up from his seat and readies his briefcase to go. He turns to me and smiles again, like the smile of a cardboard cutout.

"Before the sun went missing," he says, in a whisper, "Dr. Higley was helping me with my project. He was helping me build a city on the surface of the sun."

Del lifts his briefcase as the train doors open at the end of the platform.

"But then the sun went missing," says Del. "Then the sun went missing."

And within a minute, Del disappears through the closing doors and the train continues on its way to the next station. Station after station pass outside the windows until I notice *Hippocampus* appear way off in the distance. The train makes another sudden curve and juts away from it, and I can tell that the neighborhood of *Hippocampus* no longer holds any rail lines. The neighborhood of *Hippocampus* has been split entirely from the rest of *the Mind*, only through ruptures and empty space does it extend towards the train.

At the next stop, I get off and start walking in its direction. Through miles, I step over cracked and gnarled pavement, roads that cut off suddenly. Something has gone *awry* here most certainly, I think to myself, *the Mind* has been split from its past.

The sun has been forgotten, I mutter now, to no one, or to myself, or to the empty stretches of space that line the roads on the way to memory. On the way to memory, the roads are lined and riddled in pockets of empty space. Holes in *the Mind* where thoughts seep through, where room is made for time to disappear.

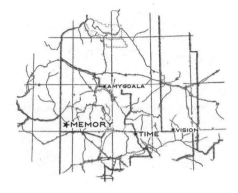

Inactive flow voids are located within
Hippocampus, long-term memory storage.

X.

THE NEIGHBORHOOD IS AN ISLET FLOATING AT THE CENTER OF *THE MIND*

A NEIGHBORHOOD APPEARS in the distance, but it's been split from the rest of the city. For miles, it's surrounded by nothing but space. Nothing but roads buckling and bending in on themselves—places where pavement once ran, now no longer.

What sort of catastrophe has occurred here, I don't know. What sort of quake or disturbance has caused a rupture in this place is unclear to me. But I can see, in the gaps and fissures of the roads that once ran here, that some sort of disturbance must have shook this place, must have caused *the Mind* to separate from its memory.

And soon, at the center of *Hippocampus*, a parking lot appears and I find myself standing in the middle of it. I'm standing in the middle of a parking lot and a car pulls up next to me, rolling down its window.

"You forgot something," says a woman inside, reaching down and grabbing an envelope.

○

"You forgot this in the diner," she says, and I turn around and notice a diner there, just like the diner I'd seen in Tempe, but half as clear and farther away.

I pocket the envelope and look around. The parking lot extends for yards in each direction, reaching out towards the desert like a memory floating in space. From the center, the parking lot seems to expand for miles even, an edgeless floating thing, the way a memory might seem from the middle of it.

"You're not from here," says the woman, ashing her cigarette against the side of the car. A small plume of smoke rises into the air and dissipates, turning into a shape that resembles a bow.

She takes her foot off the brake and another plume shoots out the back of her car. It rises into the air and forms a cloud that disperses. Like a neurochemical release, it rises and disperses in the air, until it's vacated from memory.

The parking lot is full of this, full of cars releasing absent signals into the air. Signals that are lost and transmuted into noise.

"*The Mind* underwent a shock recently," says the woman, glancing over. "A month ago, something happened here."

She taps her cigarette and a few ashes fall to the ground.

"That's why the sun's gone missing," she says. "Because something happened."

The parking lot glistens with a strange heat, and the ashes from the woman's cigarette meld into the pavement and glisten up there.

"Before the sun disappeared," says the woman. "*The Mind* underwent a strange incident."

She blows another ring of smoke, which transforms into an octagon, then a shape I've never seen before. A shape that's less of a shape and more of a mood, a movement of thought in abstract space.

And soon the parking lot becomes like this. Less like a discrete place and more like a mood moving through it. Like a series of shapes that are impossible to determine, that seem to change upon second glance.

The woman's car makes a revving sound and the ground rumbles below it with a tremor. I notice it shake my feet and reorient me.

"Do you know who *M* is?" says the woman now, staring at me coolly.

M, I mutter.

"Yes," I say, looking up. "*M* is someone I loved."

The woman nods and looks over at me.

"Something happened with *M*," she says. "A month ago."

The woman blows another ring.

"Something happened, and now *the Mind* forgets."

M, I mutter, looking up at the woman, who takes another drag and turns the tip of her cigarette red. She taps it against the side of the car and continues.

"What happened to *M*?" I say, and the woman outs her cigarette on the ground.

"That's just it," she says. "I don't remember."

My throat drops down into the cavity of my chest. I feel

it drop there for a moment and no sound can stomach its way up to me. No words form and I feel the cavity of my breath. *M*, I want to mutter, but can muster no form of sound. I want to mutter, *of course, M*, but the words can't find their way to my throat.

"Forgetting is a defense against shock."

Without warning, the woman taps the gas and disappears just the same way she had in Tempe, without a trace. And before long, her car disappears into the blind horizon of memory. Before long, her car disappears past the edge of the parking lot.

M, I mutter, and wonder where she is, and why I'd forgotten her. *Why had I forgotten M?* I think to myself, and remember now, the envelope in my back pocket, so I go to grab it.

I squint down and see it there—*From M*—written on the front.

I tear open the sealing to see what's inside, what note *M* has to deliver from an unclear distance, but as I do, I'm not sure what's there.

I stare down at the paper and turn it over, and over again,

confused, because as I look at it, there's nothing written on the note at all. The message is entirely blank.

M, I mutter, and wonder what's missing now. Why is there nothing written on the note? Does *M* have nothing more to say? Or are her words simply lost, sent through an invisible chasm?

If it were possible, I'd write a letter of my own, telling *M* exactly where I am, and that I'm looking. But if she found it, I'm not sure she'd even know my words were meant for her. *Is that you, M?* I'm not sure she'd recognize her own name.

Donna Summer's voice drifts from a car across the parking lot.

> *Someone found a letter you wrote me,*
> *on the radio*
> *And they told the world just*
> *how you felt*

The car circles by.

> *It must have fallen out of a hole*
> *In your old brown overcoat*

They never said your name
But I knew just who they meant

I stare back down at the empty note in my hand, but there's nothing there. No trace of words on the page at all, as blank as a fresh sheet of paper. I fold it over into a square and pocket it again, and watch as the parking lot becomes dimmer. I stand there for a while, looking out over blank space, and without a movement, or a car or a train, I find myself going elsewhere in the city. Soon, without moving, I find myself in a familiar crevice of thought, a neighborhood with a small library at the center of it, *Wernicke's Area*, and I climb up the steps to walk inside, into the musty smell of a dark room.

The voice of a librarian carries through it, in a murmur, though it's hard to tell through the dark shadows of the hall.

"Listen closely, because I'm speaking directly to you."

Receptive aphasia observed in subject; correlates reduced
transmission in posterior convolution of *Wernicke's Area*.

XI.
WERNICKE'S
AREA

"WHEN A WORD is written, it's fast asleep. It's tucked beneath the covers of a book and resting there silently."

○

"That's the difference between written and spoken words. Spoken are meant for somebody *who's there*. But written are silent, waiting for someone who isn't there, someone who will read them later, but who knows where, and who knows if ever. A book is always sleeping, always waiting for someone who isn't there."

○

"I've been here for many years now, in this library, tending to the books and stacks. Every day I scan the rows and check to make sure everything is in order. That each book is in the right place, and that its spine and lining haven't begun to deteriorate."

○

"Sometimes I find notes tucked between the pages of books. Secret messages passed between strangers, and whenever I find such a note, I make sure to remove it, to throw it away. My job is to maintain the integrity of the collection here, which, as you can see, is quite large in scale."

○

"And every now and again, when time permits, I'll slip open the pages of a book and begin to read it. I consider this part of my job as well. Though it may seem unnecessary, I find that opening the pages of books helps maintain their longevity. For whatever reason, I find that the act of opening a book actually prolongs its life."

○

"A month ago, I was in the stacks, and I opened a book as I tend to do, and I noticed something different with one of the pages. I placed it back and opened another book, and then another, and I noticed the same peculiarity that I'd noticed in the first. It was subtle, so I couldn't quite make sense of it at the time, but as my mind came around to it, I realized that the words, the ones I'd read, no longer made any sense.

I would read a sentence of language, and at the end of it, I'd have nothing in my head. I'd have no thought whatsoever, no way to piece back the logic of the line."

○

"Mind you, the words were still there on the page. The same letters as before, the same arrangement. But suddenly none of them meant anything. None of them added up. It was as if each word had been plucked of its meaning. Just shapes on a page pointing nowhere."

○

"So I continued to read the books. I'd flip them open and scan through, because of course, this is my job. To maintain the collection. And I figure, as long as the books are being opened, their spines will stay intact, their linings straight and sturdy. But each day, I noticed the same phenomenon. That the words only worked as shapes. And I read them that way, as abstract figures, as a language that could only communicate through form."

○

"The running motion of the river *r*, the dotted *i* and valley *v*. When I came across the word *s-u-n*, it stared me straight between the eyes. Only reason I knew the word was in fact *sun* was because I drew it with my hand. This is where it starts to get strange."

○

"As I read these books, I began drawing on a pad of notepaper next to them. I'd draw with my left hand as my eyes scanned the page, and to my surprise, I'd look over and see what I'd scribbled. If the word *b-i-r-d* appeared in a book, I'd look over and see a *bird* drawn on the notebook paper. Another word, I'd look over and see I'd scribbled it there, to my surprise. So somehow, on a certain level, I was aware of what the words were pointing to. But my active mind, the one scanning the page, had no clue what any of the words meant. They were just shapes, lines suggesting a form but nothing beyond it."

○

"When the word *s-u-n* appeared, I looked over at the pad and saw that I'd drawn *a sun* there. That my left hand had recognized the word and rendered it apart from the book. This struck me, because I hadn't seen the sun in days then, not even in a drawing. There were no images of the sun that had crossed me since it disappeared, until this moment, until I saw that I'd scribbled it next to me on paper."

○

"*What could it mean?* I thought. That my mind could no longer render the word *s-u-n* but that my left hand had. That it had known what my eyes had seen, even though my mind had no clue whatsoever. It led me to suspect that maybe the sun was still hidden somewhere, but that the path to it was out of my control. That the sun could still be found, but that the only way towards it would be circuitous."

○

"So I kept doing this, reading the senseless words and drawing them with my left hand. And eventually, I'd filled the entire pad with drawings and moved on to a new one. But the drawing of the sun lingered in my head. Even when I left the library at night, to go home and sleep, I'd see its image as I closed my eyes for bed. I'd see it there, and when I woke up in the morning, it would be there again. Something about the drawing was trying to communicate a message to me, but I couldn't figure it out. I couldn't understand what the drawing was trying to say. Until just a few days ago, it dawned on me that the drawing of the sun was pointing somewhere, to some part of *the Mind* the sun had disappeared to."

○

"Of course, the sun had disappeared from memory. I couldn't remember it. And it had disappeared from language. Words no longer meant anything. But the *image* of the sun was still somewhere, it must have been, because my hand had remembered how to draw it. So then I realized, it was *vision*. The sun must be hidden somewhere it could be *seen*. Even though

I couldn't remember it, or read the word on a page, the image still made sense."

A library materializes out of nothing, like eyesight flickering on. From the rafters, a stack of books comes staggering down into its shadow, and everywhere the library extends, the walls are papered over in rows of books. Rows and stackings of books and encyclopedias in various stages of wear.

From a few feet away, the voice of the librarian carries towards me, and I see him standing there, an older man tucked into the waistline of his pants. He stares at me through a pair of wide-rimmed glasses, which turn his eyes the same size as his face.

"Can you see me?" he says, squinting forward, and I nod. The librarian adjusts his glasses and squints again.

○

"What are you doing?" he asks, and I mutter something. The librarian smiles and nods again. "It's the sun," he says, smiling. "You're after the sun, that's why you're here."

He turns and signals with his hand. *Follow me*, he mutters, and the two of us walk to the back of the library, then down a long flight of stairs twisting into the bowels of the basement. The stairs wind down and down further, much farther than I'd imagined the library could go, and by the time we get to the bottom, the librarian opens the door to a room and we walk inside.

It's quiet in there, and when the librarian shuts the door, a wide hush falls over the entire space. I look around and dimly see a row of books wrap fully across the wall, forming an odd kind of soundproofing.

I start to speak but notice my voice get muffled immediately in the air, my words taken from the room and flattened into silent book letters. The librarian starts to speak as well, but his voice is muffled too, lost in the thickness of the air and gone silent. As he speaks, all I see is the movement of his mouth, his throat and tongue forming the shape of words, but most of them evade me.

Can you hear? he mutters silently, and I shake my head no. The librarian adjusts his glasses and repeats the question, still no sound.

After another back-and-forth, he nods to himself slightly, then turns to the wall and takes down a book, leaving it flat open on a table before me. He points to the cover page, and I look over his shoulder to see what's there, but the words are impossible to decipher. I look straight at them, but they appear as a foreign alphabet might.

An entire paragraph of nonsense, of letters shaped like arrows and holes—like knots and wires configured in arbitrary loops. For a moment, a word resembles something I know, but with the movement of a line, it changes meaning completely.

What language is this? I ask.

Eventually the librarian shifts the page to something near the back, a diagram I can make sense of—a depiction of the solar system, with the planets orbiting around the middle, but in the very middle, there's nothing—there's a spot where the sun is missing. I look up at the librarian, and he mutters a word, but again, it's lost in the stacks.

Sun, I see him mutter, I think. *Sun*, he says, and then I look down and realize we're reading *Dr. Higley's* book.

This is in another language, I say. I read a line, but the words fall like wrong notes in a scale. I see a word, but as soon as my mind begins to process it, the word itself changes into something else. A word that looks like the word but means another thing entirely. *Sun. Sum. Son. Some.*

I flip back to the diagram and stare at it. I stare at the spot where the sun should be and see a small piece of silver foil there—a crinkled dot of foil—and I stare down at it, noticing something forming in the reflection. I stare down at the central dot, squinting my eyes and noticing the reflection of something shimmering back.

An eye, I mutter.

I look up at the librarian, but he's staring down too. He's staring at the diagram.

An eye, I mutter, leaning closer, and I see it there, a singular eye reflected back from the silver dot—a round iris and pupil staring up from the foil. *Whose eye is this?* I think, and continue to stare down at the silver reflection.

It's not my own, I know. It can't be, because no matter how far forward or backward I lean, the reflection of the eye remains the same. Even if I squint up close to the silver foil, the reflection of the eye maintains the same distance. As if someone were staring at me through the pages of the book.

What is this? I mutter, but the librarian remains focused on the page and doesn't look up. *What does this mean?* I say.

I try to read the caption below the diagram, but the words point me in no direction. Still the eye remains staring from the center of the page. Not my own, but an eye reflected up. *Could it be Dr. Higley's? But how?* And soon, the longer I think, the contents of my thoughts themselves become muted. I can hardly hear the words forming within my own head. The words form and become immediately dim, immediately harder to decipher, until all of them are nonsense, until none of them can be heard.

And soon, all I can see is the eye at the center, the solar

system circled around it. I squint down and bring my face even closer, as close as I can possibly go to the foil, until it's my entire field of vision, the silver foil and the eye reflected up. I get so close that the iris disappears and all I see is the reflection of the pupil, the black hole worming down into the depths of the page, the book descending into the folds of the cover. I see through the bottom of the reflection, lower and lower and lower, like the stairs down into the bowels of the basement, and eventually, after what feels like a minute, I lift my head up and look back at the page. I stare down at it, at the words there, which come suddenly into focus, which make sense to me all at once. But now, as I squint at the foil, I notice nothing is there—the eye is missing—only silver shimmering up.

What is this? I mutter, and hear my voice echo from the walls, which are cleared of books somehow. The shelves are empty, and soon I can hear myself clearly in the chambers of the room. "What is this?" I say, looking down at the diagram, and then up at the librarian.

But now the librarian stares at me with his glasses off. He stares at me and points to his eye. He points to his eye and mutters something.

"Go inside," he says, pointing to his left eye and shutting it closed.

"Go inside," he says, and without warning, I'm elsewhere in *the Mind*.

XII.
IN A PIT
OF THOUGHT,
A NEIGHBORHOOD
COLLAPSES
INTO BLINDNESS

IN A REGION of the city *Amygdala*, space collapses into a dark cloud where nothing can be seen. Space can only be described through the senses of touch and feel, the odd texture of a knotted loop, a glossy surface turning cool under the pressure of a hand.

A groove in *the Mind*'s surface opens up, and I move inside, into the tactile geometry of emotional space. A numb sense takes hold of me there and pulls me lower, into a realm of feeling below, a space carved out through darkness. In the corner, a shadow moves in a familiar shape. Without seeing, I know who it is.

M, I mutter, and reach out, but my hand catches no surface. *M*, I say, as my voice is lost in sound. The walls of feeling send no echo back to me, only the shape of the letter in my mouth, *M*.

I begin moving towards her, but as I do, the logic of space unfolds. The linearity of motion begins to falter, and as I move towards *M*, I find myself falling farther away, farther towards a layer of darkness below, a nook carved out by a hollow edging of thought. *M*, I say, and fall farther and farther into darkness, into a realm where even the knowledge of sight can't be found.

A hollow note carries through my sternum and turns into a shape below my throat. *Oh*, I want to say, but no sound carries, and the feeling is trapped in a trochlear nerve, in the shallow spot below my opening.

Oh, I want to call, and fall in through the hollow note of that sound, *O*, that senseless shape. But as I try to move through it, a numbness folds above my throat and keeps me there. *O*, I think, and feel that openness hollow itself lower into my sternum and below.

A cool sensation stirs around me and pulls my lungs into a tangled knot, into a shape that makes no sense for a body in space. I try edging my way out, towards the memory *M*, but she's nowhere in sight. I'd like to know where she is, I think, but as soon as I do, my body descends another layer, until I'm surrounded by total blindness.

The cavity in my chest grows some more, and I sink farther inside. Until I locate the source of the aching, a spot just below my sternum, like a hole in the sky where the sun was, now gone. I fall into that open space and stay there for as long as I can. *Oh*, I want to say, and swallow the sound of that note, that hollow numbness that carries through my body and keeps me there. *I want to go*, I think. I want to move through the darkness of this space and arrive on the other end, arrive on the spot where *M* is, but motion no longer makes sense. The logic of feeling tangles me further into a knot, and I twist into a shape I can't recognize, into that window whose wind carries through my chest and buries me.

M, I mutter, as my mouth turns to water, as the water falls through the drain of my pipes and stays there as wind. *M*, I say, but now she's nowhere around, not even the memory of her shadow is near me.

I imagine the sky. Imagine tumbling through it, and that blind spot there. That hole where the sun once was, now a wound. Now an open mark emitting no light, only a blinding shell in all directions.

And I can feel that hole in my chest, that spot where something went missing. Like the sun from the sky, I can feel that hole in my chest where the memory *M* once was, now gone. That empty note, and I lower into it, sinking towards the blind heat of its absence. That shape forming *O* just inside my sternum, like the loss of meaning. *Oh gOd*, I say, and fall through the hollow shape of those hollow words, *oh* and *god*, those empty forms that carry only a sound for me now. That carry no sound in the walls of feeling, but a shape in space, a haptic form of sensation.

M, I mouth, and feel the magnetic pull of that spot deepen, that missing link below my core. The outline of a form, *M*, and I lose myself in it. A swelling pain stirs around me, and I go inside, tangling into a knot that curls inward towards an unrecognizable form. A pain I hadn't known until now, and now I fall towards it. Crashing into that open window whose wind drags me inward.

A thought passes. And without another hesitation, I'm thrown down into that gutter, that hole carved through the center of *Solar Plexus*, the cluster of nerves located at the bottom of the heart mind. No longer in the brainscape but in the body, in the cluster of nerves radiating from the core, from the heart muscle at the center of feeling. Through the hollow note of missing, I fall into that spot below my sternum, into that hole sewn through the middle of the heart, like the hole in the sky, I move through it, and I'm there.

M, I mutter.

XIII.
AND AT THE CENTER
OF THE HEART,
A MEMORY ARISES
THROUGH THE
HEAT OF FEELING

FROM THE DEPTHS of *Solar Plexus*, an image emerges, appearing through the shifting glass of refracted time.

In a home we both lived in, I see *M* lying there, in the middle of a carpeted floor dyed jade with lamplight. She's lying there sideways, and her eyes are torn from the pages of a book which she holds open in her left hand.

M, I mutter, seeing her face clearly now. Her two eyes stare up at me, exactly as eyes would, as two balls of light reflecting the bright color of the room. I can see the rest of her face too, her nose and mouth made equally bright from the lampshade.

A metal stud appears through the upper portion of her right eyebrow, and I notice a small metal ball at the end of it, like a disco ball reflecting the bright light of the room and sending it in fractals across the wall. The house is exactly as I remembered it, except that there isn't any furniture around, just the carpeted floor and the lampshade in the corner.

I look at *M* and see her look up at me. Her face appears clearly once again. Below her left eye, I notice the lines of an ink tattoo traced in a small familiar shape. A line marking the image of a luna moth, a scattering of dots strewn across the back of its wings like decoy eyes, like a form of camouflage to distract predators. *Moth*, I mutter, and watch it change shape in the reflection of light from the corner. *M* blinks and a memory comes surfacing back through the refraction of space. *M and I lived in this house*, I remember now. *We lived here together some time ago.*

I lean down and bend myself closer towards her. The texture of carpet on my hand creates the sensation of sinking, of falling deeper into feeling and out of thought. Into the warm clutches of felt memory, that old surface whose edges have no hem. For a moment, sight eludes the space around me, and I fall into that warm spot below my heart again, *Solar Plexus*, the center of the peripheral nervous system.

○

I remember, *M* flew planes.

○

M was a pilot.

○

When I met *M*, she'd just begun to fly professionally. She flew a plane called the *Bumble Bee*, because of the sound it made whenever she took off. From land I could hear *M's* plane buzzing through the sky, disappearing into clouds and then shuttling away.

We lived next to a small airport. Most days, I worked from home for a company that paid me to sleep. They paid me to sleep during the day, I remember, and perform experiments on my dreams, and when *M* came home at night from flying, the two of us would sit over a bowl of soup and think of something to talk about—whatever it was I'd dreamed that day, or wherever it was she'd flown to.

Sometimes it wasn't soup but a vegetable, or a cut of steak. *M* and I ate steak in those days, I remember. We'd cook it simply with some salt and butter, sometimes mustard, and throw it on the stove for a few minutes.

M lived in the sky. Even when we were home, I could tell her mind was always halfway through the clouds, which was funny, because I was the same way. I was always halfway there and halfway in a dream.

At a certain point, I remember I started having this dream about *M's* plane. It would start the same way—*M* taking off in the *Bumble Bee* and rising into the clouds. I'd see her jet disappear into the sky and fly farther and farther away, until somehow I knew deep down that she was never coming back.

The first time I had the dream, it frightened me. And I told *M* about it, but she smiled and said *don't worry*. Still the dream persisted, almost every day I'd see *M's* plane in my sleep and wonder if she was ever coming home. At night, when she returned, I'd tell her again, and she'd say not to worry.

Eventually the dreams became more and more realistic. For instance, if I saw *M's* plane take off and head west, just by coincidence, *M* would tell me that she *had* flown west that day. Or if I saw her plane leave a hole in a cloud, she would say that was odd, because she *had* flown through a cloud that day. Each night, the dreams became more and more realistic, and I began to worry that I was scaring *M* away with them. That somehow my fear would come true, and that *M* would leave because of these terrible feelings.

One morning, *M* left for the airport, and I went to bed. I drifted off to sleep, and in my dream, I saw the *Bumble Bee* rise into the sky, flying off farther and farther into the distance, then disappearing. Again, I knew that *M* wasn't coming back. That evening, when it was time for *M* to come home, she didn't. I waited by the door, but as the hours went on, I knew my dream had sent her away, that she was never returning.

I couldn't tell if my fear had come true or if I was still somehow sleeping. I couldn't tell if *M* had really left, or if I was lost in a delusion of my own. Regardless, when *M* went away, the sun did too. When *M*'s plane disappeared into the sky, she took the memory of its light with her.

○

I look across the carpet and see *M* lying there now, through the fractured lines of remembered sight. Through a frame of memory, the moth on her cheek winks in the fuchsia shade of the shifting room tone. From jade to copper, to a warmer color infused with red.

I miss you, I mutter, and *M* looks over at me.

I bend down and lower myself closer towards her, knee to knee on the floor. Still she notices my attention with a slight delay, as though I'm not quite there, or as though my motion is coded through a filter of time I can't see.

I miss you, I say again, pushing my voice through the density of space, through the filter of distance between us. Outside, a sprinkler begins its rotation. *M* looks up at me and blinks. She traces her hand along the sides of my face.

You look tired, she says, staring at the lines below my eyes.

The lighting in the room turns softer somehow. And in its softness, *M* becomes even more visible. I can see her skin glimmer in its own heat, in the heat of the force embodied beneath it.

I know, I mutter, and time comes fluttering back through the folded channels of thought. Through the image of *M* before me, like a reflection I'd forgotten, I can see the shape of the past month form itself in retrospect. *I know*, I say, and feel my heart again, that spot below my sternum, *Solar Plexus*, rise with the warm heat of remembered feelings.

I stare at *M*, and the delay shortens. The space between us grows less dense, less fogged in a filter of time. *Where did you go?* I ask now, and wait for my words to travel a few feet towards her. She folds the book over, shutting it closed, then stares up at me as the sprinkler continues its rhythm.

Nowhere, she says.

And the lighting in the room turns to a deeper fuchsia. The knot in my chest loosening into a warmer color, into a looser shape—an untangled bow, a ribbon untying.

I've always been right here, she says, looking straight at me through the filter of time. *Right here, as always.*

The sprinkler turns towards the window and sprays a thin mist through the opening in the glass, wetting the carpet slightly and landing on our feet. Neither of us flinches, and the sprinkler turns away again, facing the rest of the lawn. I smile at the ground, and *M* does too, the delay erased momentarily, the two of us in the same space without much of a filter in between.

I want to fall into the crooks of your form, I say, and *M* leans down to invite me towards her, the border of her shirt lifting above her waist, so that I can see what's there below, the dark furrows of her parted legs.

I reach down and run my hand along the carpeted floor, the pink lamplight in the corner tracing my movements with its shadow, as I fall towards the heat of *M*, the clustered nerves of *Solar Plexus*.

M, I mutter, and buckle forward, falling between the stalks of her shape, into the old form filtered through the heat of missing. *M*, I mutter, and forget myself. Even more, I forget myself until I'm the fuchsia color turning red inside of my veins, the warm heat rising within me like the lampshade turning deeper, like the movement of blood coursing.

M, I say, and she moves away for a moment, retreating to the far corner of the room where the lighting is even dimmer than here. For a moment, she faces away, and my heart turns into the O shape of longing, into the old question of closeness and proximity.

From the other side of the room, I see *M's* shirt falling just below her, just past the lower part of her waist, and for a brief moment, I'm stuck on the other end, sinking into the loose texture of the carpet.

M removes her shirt now so I can see her back clearly in the lamplight of the opposite corner. Though dimmer, I see her muscles from across the way—she turns around again and faces me, standing some distance above now, her body a blazing sign of what I'd forgotten, of what had been buried deep in the clusters of dark muscle.

M, I say, and fall between the mounds of her chest, the deep basin of forgotten feeling, of a body I'd so longed to know again. And just as simply, the space between us dissolves and I'm there, fallen between her memory, between the shape whose outline had lost itself inside me and gone, and turned into the hole of longing, the hole of forgotten light.

I step back an inch and look at *M*, noticing the tattoo under her left eye shift in the falling light. Like a pair of eyes itself, the dots on the back of its wings blink in the shifting tone of the fuchsia room color. In the color of a fuchsia room, *M* is smiling at me with a warmth that I'd only thought could exist in retrospect, laughing at some expression come over my face.

I laugh and fall backwards, *M* falling over me as well, the two of us folding into a crisscrossed braid on the floor. As *M* sits up again, the pronouncement of her swelling breasts come fully into view, like two round words forming at the ends of speech.

My tongue takes a trip across the sound they make, the shape they form along the roof of my mouth, my lips and tongue opening to allow a note to come out, to carve a space in which a sound can form—*God*—*Oh*—I mutter, and fall inside the depths of that sound, that lowest exclamation.

A bird flitters outside and makes a sharp noise. The combination of its sound and the sprinkler conspire to produce a feeling within me that swells in an unbearable niceness, a memory too sweet to recall without falling into its grasp.

The sprinkler turns, and I'm back on my side. I'm twisted into a shape with *M* on the floor, the two of us combined in a knot of tangled nerves, in a ball of rising pressure. *M*, I mutter, and feel the wetness of the ground, the sprinkler turned once again in our direction, spraying our legs and feet to no mind, to no bother of thought. The two of us tangle back, and the sprinkler switches sides, so we roll across the ground and end up crosswise.

My cock tightens, and I feel *M* between me. I feel the rising pressure of potential surging towards the heights of its threshold, a flood of ions rushing across their gradient. As the potential narrows, I sense *M* below me, her tightness increasing as well, the pressure of heat rising from her body like a cluster of nerves radiating from the core, like the warmth of the sun expanding evenly and outward.

In the moment of apex, a warm glow expands across the space of the living room, a bright release of energy escaping the space between us, and within us, like the heat of the sun returned once again and in clear sight. The sun returned again, as if its heat were never missing.

The sprinkler shuts off, and the floor is wet in its aftermath. I stare at *M*, and she laughs. The two of us laugh as though no month had past, as though we had always been right there, in the same spot as always. But of course, we both know the joke, which is that *M* is not there at all, that she's as missing as she's always been. Her image leaves the living room as soon as it was there.

And like that, the memory of her closeness lingers like a stinging thought, like something unbearably bright to handle. Too close now, I think, the memory of that sweetness now lost, that unbearable comfort whose contours are burnished and faded.

And from the heights of that feeling, a sorrow singes me down into the tunnels of darkness, into the blindness of that spot from which I came. For what seems like more than a minute, or an hour, I'm there again in that shadowed hole, that cornered mess of swaddled nerves—a spot lower than any other buried deeper, a wound prodded open and dragged below.

In that location of shock, that space with no language at all, I go farther inside, into the rupture of space where time ceases to pass through me. No word can form in the blindness of that region, in the searing pain of its weight.

And from the darkness of feeling in the pits of sorrow, an image appears as if through a tunnel's well. A mirage rising at the end of eyesight, like a vision formed to evade a more inconceivable pain. A vision in the distance, *Optic Cortex*, and I go into its sedating light.

And a town appears, an image just like Sun City.

VISION

XIV.
DEL WEBB SITS
BEHIND HIS DESK ATOP
A CLOCKTOWER

IN A TOWN that appears almost exactly like Sun City,
a clocktower rises into the air from the center, a few stories
taller than the buildings around it. From the center, where a
parking lot was, a tower rises into the air, and Del Webb sits
inside it, in an office carved into the apparatus of a clock.

The room is a small rotunda whose walls are overlaid in
a series of television screens, and at the center, Del Webb sits
in his chair, watching.

The office flips upside down for a moment—then my vision corrects itself so that everything is right side up again.

"The idea with Sun City," says Del below his breath,
muttering to himself. "Was to build a city where the sun

was always there, where the sky was always bright at any hour of the night or day. The only way to do this was to build a city on the sun itself, to build a city the sun would never leave."

From the television screens, footage of a security apparatus appears, each Sun City from various overhead angles. On one screen in particular, a panoramic image of Arizona, and through the window of a one-story home, the silhouette of a man lying fast asleep in bed.

"Dr. Higley is in a dream now," mutters Del quietly, staring up at the screens. His vision seems entwined with them somehow, the movement of their glow paralleling the movement of his thoughts exactly. "Dr. Higley is in a dream," he says. "And in his dream, he's in *the Mind*."

A wave of light moves across the room and bends in a chromatic aberration—violet—blue—before returning to white again.

"Dr. Higley was helping me with my project. He was helping me build my city on the sun. But as soon as we began construction, it disappeared. The sun disappeared as soon as we took our first measurements."

Del stays seated in his chair, his eyes fixed in place, captivated by the same bright image.

"You know, it's the strangest thing," says Del, unmoving in his seat. "But just the other night, I received a telephone call."

Del turns and stares down at a small wooden telephone propped atop his desk, silver cord, plastic, coiled.

"I received a voice mail on this telephone from Dr. Higley just the other evening."

Del says nothing, muttering a word to himself.

"How is that possible?" I say. "Isn't Dr. Higley asleep?"

"I received a voice message on *this* telephone," repeats Del, pointing to the receiver, then staring up at the white glow of the screens. "And in the message, Dr. Higley told me something about the sun's location. In the message, Dr. Higley said the sun was hidden in plain sight. But that the problem with *sight* is it's impossible to see. One can see anything in the world, expect for *vision* itself. One can see anything except for the spot from which one looks."

◯

"The sun is there, he said, in the blind spot at the center of vision."

The red light on the telephone receiver blinks on and off.

"Where is that?" I ask.

Del says nothing, studying the monitors whose light washes over him, turning his face softer, anesthetized by its soothing glow. I see him wince slightly, almost unnoticeably, before returning blank.

"I miss the sun," says Del now, whispering to himself. "But you know, I think what we have these days is better. Who needs the sun when you have Sun City?"

A light moves across the room and splits into static, into a small dust storm carrying across empty space. Outside, the clocktower makes a noise that carries across the length of the town that appears just like Sun City. Del winces again, as his eyes stay glued to the screen.

"Please don't go," he mutters below his breath, his hand

tracing the telephone wire beside him. "Don't leave," he says without shifting his tone, without moving his face in any direction at all.

Soon the screens before him glow so sharply that they fill the room with their light, until the walls of the office dissolve and I'm elsewhere, transported to another optic region of *the Mind*, a set of nerves and a railroad track, a train headed through the middle of the desert, splitting the sand left and right across it.

In the middle of the desert, a train track appears and I'm on it, headed in some direction forward, some vaster landscape of vision.

"Don't go," whispers Del.

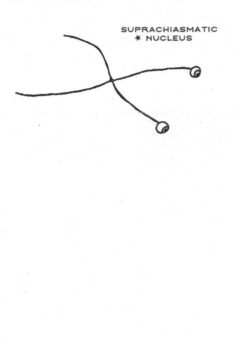

★OPTIC CORTEX

SUPRACHIASMATIC
★ NUCLEUS

XV.
A TRAIN MOVES
THROUGH
THE DESERT BLIND

GOD IS ALIVE *again.*

I feel the presence of something around me now, some inarticulable shape forming blind traces of desert sight. As the train moves forward, the desert forms around it.

I find myself less interested in the shapes of desert space than in the pockets that stretch around them. Not in the stems or branches of tissue, but the gaps of room in between, the fissures and ventricles that shape the absence of thought.

The absence of thought moves the train through the desert. The space recedes just as soon as it's there, just enough to let it through. The train moves the way light does, through the desert without sound.

And without a sound, without so much as a passing whistle, the train moves through the various regions of vision within *the Mind*, *Superior Colliculus*, down through *Cuneus* and *Optic Radiation*. A wink of neon sneaks off the back of a pair of saguaros, where an optic cable carries blue, yellow from the cones to the *Cortex*.

Inside the train, no sound moves at all through the cabin. No motion stirs, and no one is aboard besides myself, no other long-distance travelers as far as I can tell.

Inside a silent cabin, I look out the window and watch the sand pile into new shapes, saguaros transmorphing into catclaw and ocotillo, palo verde, prickly pear. At each gap junction, a pulse moves from one nerve ending to another, from one train track to the next, sending a hidden message just beneath the surface of sand, a movement of color pulsing beneath the layers of dirt and rock that populate the face of the desert.

The nature of *the Mind* is the nature of nature, I now see. That the shapes of thought are the same ones as space, that an idea might move just as light would, or a soft wind across sand.

As the train rolls on, I look down in my seat and see a table there with a telephone resting atop it, stretching silver cord, like the one in the clocktower except now moving at high speed through the desert.

To my surprise, the phone begins to ring, so I pick up the call but no one's there at the other end of the line. I place the phone back down then look out the window, as the light replicates itself through space, blue to yellow then back again, each color replacing its opposite—as soon as red appears, cyan is there to take its place, and so on in reverse, a series of colors moving in mimetic succession.

Again, I look down and hear the phone ringing, so I pick up the receiver and press it firmly against my ear. This time I hear a voice on the other end, vaguely, though any sound is almost impossible to make out. I listen some more but still can't hear whoever it is, and eventually I place the receiver back down.

In my pocket, I notice the envelope there, the blank note I'd received outside the diner. I fold it open and stare at the blank page, but somehow, as I stare down, I see something written at the center of the blank note—a few digits scribbled, a phone number, which I press onto the light oak dialing pad of the telephone before me, and without speaking, a voice answers on the other end of the line.

Without a sound, I know exactly who it is.

The train turns towards the middle of the desert. In that moment, a boy's voice comes clearly down the receiver. On the other end of the line, I hear the boy who sunk to the bottom of the pool in Tempe speaking, the star of his high school swim team.

"I had a feeling the other day that I might receive a telephone call like this, at this exact hour, and that whoever was calling, a stranger, I wouldn't know him, but I would tell him something about what happened to me that morning the sun disappeared, that morning I forgot how to swim and sank to the bottom of the varsity pool. Now of course the sky was black that morning when I awoke, because the sun wasn't there yet, it hadn't risen. And at six on the dot, I went to school and changed into my swim trunks, took a cold shower, dried off, and when I got out, I looked in the mirror, and I saw myself there, and I saw myself there again—for some reason the morning the sun went missing, I was seeing everything twice. When I got to the pool, I saw my teammates, but each one was two versions of themselves, two swim trunks, two goggles per pair. Now that's where my memory blanks out. I can hardly remember jumping in the water that morning. I can hardly remember anything up until I had sunken to the bottom of the pool, until I found myself standing at the deep end with my feet on the tiles. Now I don't know how long I was there, submerged underwater, and I don't know what I thought when I opened my eyes and realized I could no longer swim, that my legs no longer knew how to move through the alien substance of *h-two-o*. So without trying to move, I stood there and resigned myself to sinking, to falling deeper below the water's surface until my legs began to float, until I was looking down at a reflection below me, the water doubled. Below me, the tiles had dissolved and I could see a reflection of the swimmers above, their legs turning laps left and right, and I could see the lines along the sides of the pool denoting the edges of space. Everything was reflected below me except for the spot below myself. When I looked there, just below, I saw nothing. I saw only a shadow moving through the depths of the water. And so I stared down, and down, but I saw only darkness in place of my image, and without thinking, I knew immediately that it was the shadow of the sun below me. I knew in that moment, without thinking, that the shadow of the sun was moving below me in the pool."

But the sun has no shadow, I mutter, as the train moves forward, traveling through a patch of light that splinters into a chaotic display. I pull the phone closer to my ear and mutter something, as the cabin skips across a jagged track.

"I swear I saw it there," says the boy. "I saw the sun's shadow at the bottom of the pool. And when my friend pulled me out, when I returned to the surface, I remembered everything just as I saw it. I remembered seeing that shadow there, and knowing that it belonged to the sun."

Another scattering of light divides the train across it, a cluster of nerves carrying the outline of some image through its field of vision. A scotopic light magnified and doubled, as the sound of the telephone cuts out for a moment and comes back in. The voice on the other end, the boy from Tempe, echoes through the wire vaguely.

"And for the rest of that day, and for the rest of this month, I've been seeing everything twice. Two versions of the same image everywhere I go. And when I close my eyes, I can see that shadow moving at the bottom of water. I can picture the sun headed in some direction somewhere—when I close my eyes, I still see it as clearly as yesterday."

But how did you know it was the shadow of the sun? I mutter now into the telephone, which cuts to static, to the sound of the train tracks below me, the jagged metal shearing against the wheels of the train car. The sound cuts out once more, and the call is dropped to silence, the boy from Tempe lost on the other end of the line.

I place the phone back down and look out the window again, at a desert just like the one I'm moving through but doubled, but across a horizontal axis of symmetry. I stare out the window and see a train just like the one I'm on now, but moving towards me, the two trains meeting at a single point of decussation.

Just as I sense my train slow to a stop, I see the opposite train stop as well, the two deserts merging at *Optic Chiasm*.

The doors of the train open and I step outside, descending into the open space of the desert. Across from me, I see a man descend the steps of a train as well, a perfect double walking towards me as I walk towards him.

Dr. Higley, I mutter, and see him standing there at the crossing of the chiasm.

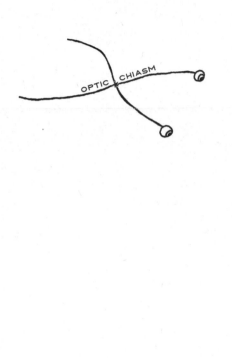

XVI.
A MAN
STANDS ACROSS
THE TRACKS

NOT IDENTICAL, BUT a double, a double version of
myself standing before me.

Dr. Higley, I mutter, and stare at the man whose name
I'd found in a newspaper and decided to call, leading mind in
the field of helioseismology. *Higley*, I mutter aloud, surprised
to see him awake, out of bed, and without an egg resting on
his forehead.

"Aren't you sleeping now?" I say in a confused voice that
carries dreamlike through desert space. "Aren't you supposed
to be asleep?" I ask again, and Dr. Higley stares up without a
moment's pause.

"I am," he replies below his breath. "I am asleep right now," he says, and I look in the corner of his eye and notice a red dot there, a small dot like a hemorrhage on the surface of his sclera.

"I am asleep. And in my dream, I'm inside of *the Mind*. I'm inside *the Mind*, and I'm speaking to you."

Dr. Higley reaches in his pocket and pulls out a small vile of teardrops, a case of droplets which he siphons into his reddened eye and the redness goes down, the dot shrinking.

The two of us stare as though left and right hemispheric doubles.

"Look up," says Dr. Higley now, without explanation, and I do. I look up in the sky and notice the bright blinding expanse of it, the harsh absence of light in the cranial abyss.

◯

"Look up in the sky and picture an eye there," he says now, seemingly without thinking, and I do again. I squint up and imagine an eye in the spot just above *Optic Chiasm*.

"*Suprachiasmatic Nucleus* is the eye above the chiasm," he says. "It's here that all the light we can't see goes."

I stare up, blinking at the center of the desert of vision.

Dr. Higley stands before me as the red dot disappears from behind the lens of his sclera, shrunken by the artificial tears in his pocket.

"Look up," he says firmly, leaning forward. "The hidden eye is there."

I stare up as though looking through a telescope, a microscope, the scope of *the Mind* extended through space, and still, I see nothing, the bright blinding absence of the sky above. I see nothing, and Dr. Higley nods.

"Of course," he says. "It's impossible to see the center of vision."

From above, the sound of buzzing swirls around my eardrum and appears on the other end in the shape of a small bee, a small worker bee buzzing around my ear and appearing before me in a visible form, then turning a loop around Dr. Higley and circling back, knotting the two of us in a series of concentric loops.

I stare at Dr. Higley and notice his attention fixed in place, in the same spot as it's been for our entire conversation. As I stare, I can tell that Dr. Higley is still asleep somehow, his vision circling a dreamlike form. At the crossing of *Optic*

Chiasm, I stare at Dr. Higley and wonder now who is really standing there, if his figure isn't simply some reflection, some dreamlike apparition of myself.

"Your eyes," Dr. Higley mutters, as if speaking from a dream. "They look tired," he says, and soon the bee turns another loop around us and disappears into the sky, into the bright fuzz of absence above. "Your eyes look red."

At a certain atmosphere, the sound of the bee and the brightness of the sky become indistinguishable, and I feel a sense of exhaustion overcome me, a weight pulling my body lower while my mind slips into the bright absence of the sky above, the unconscious eye of the sky above. Dr. Higley stands before me a statue, a projection, until a moment passes and it's unclear whether he's there at all.

SUPRACHIASMATIC
★ NUCLEUS

★OPTIC
CHIASM

XVII. ONCE AGAIN, IN A CLOCKTOWER, IN A TOWN JUST LIKE SUN CITY

A ROOM APPEARS exactly as it had before. At the top parapets of the optic apparatus, a rotunda forms again, except now, as I look around, I notice that Del Webb isn't there, that no one is sitting at the center of the security desk.

Sleeping eye, flattened sun.

Down a long flight of stairs and again in the middle of a parking lot, in the same parking lot as before, stretching outward towards the concentric grid of lines and roads marking Sun City.

A few meters ahead, the outline of a person appears with a pair of binoculars in his hands, and approaching closer, I can see that it's Del Webb, walking towards me through the middle of the parking lot. He glances up casually and mentions something about the sun, that he's looking for it too, and disappears without another word towards the far end of the lot.

As the asphalt recedes into the pavement of roads, I find myself inside a home resembling the Sun City Museum, and Martha Adie is there, Dr. Higley's wife, sitting on a couch and speaking to me as though I've been standing there for hours, as though the two of us have been deep in conversation.

"When I was just a little girl growing up in Phoenix, I used to love to listen to music. And sometimes at night when my parents were sleeping, I would sneak into the living room and listen to the radio alone at a low volume, and the music they would play at night was different from the music they would play during the day, and it was dreamlike and enchanting, and I remember I was transfixed by the sound of that old console in the parlor of my parents' home. But little by little, I would listen to the radio less and less, and as I grew older, I would hardly find myself listening to music at all, for whatever reasons, which remain mysterious to me now—as I grew older and became an adult, I stopped listening to music completely. It wasn't until just the other year, just a year or so ago, I was inside a car wash in Tempe, and a song came on the radio that was exactly like the songs I would listen to as a child growing up, and it was the same strange sound that I'd heard in my parents' home. I was alone in the car wash, I remember, and I was sitting in the waiting room watching my car go through the washer, and before the song reached even the first minute, I was entirely moved to tears, and I was crying as the song came over the speakers, because it had been so many years since I'd heard that music, and I was transported immediately to the feeling I would get as a child in Phoenix. When the song played itself through, the voice of the radio broadcaster came over the speakers, and he said the name of the musician, and I knew that whoever it was, he must be the greatest musician in the world, because his music had moved me to tears, because his music had transported me back to Phoenix, and it was *Yo-Yo Ma*."

The walls of Martha's home recede into the walls of the museum, then back again onto the streets of the ocular city.

An ever-brightening sky elevates overhead. For a moment, a thought reveals itself towards me.

The sun is the source of our senses,
and it makes no sense now.
Nonsense is the only sightline towards it.

A car passes on the street and I watch it go without a sound. And soon the eye of nonsense enunciates itself, and it makes its shape clearly seen.

Like an egg cracked open through the sky, the eye of non-sense reveals itself around me, and I'm standing on it, on an invisible eye in the spot where the sun used to be.

XVIII.
THE EYE OF NONSENSE IS AN INVISIBLE EYE ON THE SPOT WHERE THE SUN USED TO BE

AS SOON AS it's visible, it disappears. The invisible eye is impossible to see—as soon as it takes a shape, it dismantles itself. In that spot where the sun was, now a hole, now the absence of light, an invisible eye appears in the sky through the form of nonsense.

Where am I? I wonder. What is this invisible space that's meant to show myself to me? To show the site of seeing, the eye at the center of it all, *where am I?* Somewhere the sun has gone to bed and sunken into the gullies of forgetting, into the furtive tunnels that wind below the visible plane, and I follow them there, further into the nonsense of the unseen eye, the location of vision at the center of *the Mind.*

Is there anything to see here, or nothing at all? There's no edge to this space, no spot to say *ah*, there *I am*. And instead, I wind further into the maze of confusion, into the delirium of a location with no clear bounds.

The only sight line now is nonsense, is a certain sort of blind groping, a feeling towards the hyperbright absence of the spot where the sun once was. And I sense, on its surface, a city just like Sun City, a city built on the absence of what was once below it. On the absence of sight, the absence of the sun, a city erects itself like a sort of phantasm. And there I am now, walking the streets of a town that's remarkably familiar, but in the sky, on the surface of the invisible eye, and before me a door opens and inside it, Dr. Higley is there.

"The problem with the eye is that it can never see itself. It can never see the point from which it sees."

I look forward and notice Dr. Higley hunched behind his desk. He gestures for a glass of water, so I bring him one and walk closer.

"The eye only knows its own reflection, its depiction, but never the spot it's looking from."

I stare over Dr. Higley's desk and notice a book turned open to a page in the back, a universe missing its point at the center, a silver foil reflecting nothing back up.

"Look," says Dr. Higley. "I'm your eye."

I squint over the desk to see that spot on the page, the eye reflected up from the center not my own, but Dr. Higley's somehow, staring at me through an impossible mirror.

"Listen," he says, peering through the pages of his book. "There are two versions of everything. The sun in the world, and the sun in *the Mind*. The truth in the world, and the truth in *the Mind*. *You* in the world, and *you* in *the Mind*."

I look down at the hidden eye.

"I am *you* in *the Mind*. I'm the one on the other side of the eye."

I stare down and see Dr. Higley there in *Quantum Sun*.

"When one of us is here, the other is there. When one of us is in *the Mind*, the other is in the world. Except now, we're both in *the Mind*. Except now, the two of us can see each other."

An invisible eye collapses inward, and remakes itself again, invisibly.

"I'm your eye," says Dr. Higley. "I'll show you where the sun is."

Dr. Higley pauses, speaking through the lines on the page, the silent letters asleep and waiting. Around us, the invisible eye illuminates an irradiant glow, the streets of the ocular town dissolving into an invisible aura.

A bee flies by but I can't see it, only the noise of buzzing circling the space between me and the page.

"There are other ways to see," says Dr. Higley, whispering silently. "Bees know where to go without even looking, without even knowing what's before them."

As Dr. Higley speaks through the silent letters, his voice buzzes with a noise indistinguishable from the bee itself, from the electrostatic buzz just beneath the surface of the visible plane.

"Bees remember space as a series of points, as places they don't even have to see. Your path to the sun follows the bee, follows a way of looking without seeing. The sun is there, in that space that can't be seen."

From beneath the surface of the ocular town, a bright

furnace erupts with the electromagnetic glow of a color that remains invisible, that lies outside the realm of eyesight.

"Be like the bee," says Dr. Higley, as I turn the page of *Quantum Sun* over, as I close my eyes and sense a pressure build across the other side of them. "Go to honeycomb. Go without knowing where to go."

And then I see it, the bee puncturing a mark through the surface of the invisible eye, leaving a red spot behind and then escaping, and then flying off into an invisible horizon. I look around and see the last trace of the ocular town dissolve into solar heat, into a gale of pressure expanding outward from the center of the invisible eye. I turn the page over, and over once more, until Dr. Higley descends into the folds, until I find myself jolted out of *the Mind* and back into the world. And I know where the sun is now.

○

THE WORLD

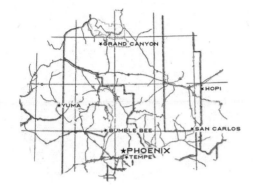

XIX.
SKY

I WAKE UP in a bed in Tempe with an egg cracked open
on my forehead.

Back in Tempe.

I look around an empty hotel room and notice a note left
on the dresser by the door. *From M*, it reads, with an address
written below. *7493 Airport Dr—Cedar City, Utah. 84721.*

And before a second thought, I climb back in the car and
hit the road up the same Arizona highway as before. Through
the same sprawling desert in the baby blue toyota I'd forgotten some time back.

Awoken with an egg on my forehead, I think, as if Dr. Higley awoken from his dream, and yet I'm not Dr. Higley, and yet I'm not sure exactly who I am.

Back in the old car, in the middle of the same Arizona highway headed north to a location in Utah where I presume *M* must live. Where *M* must be waiting.

In the rearview, I see Tempe disappear into road lines, into a highway thinning towards a double lane. And no traffic in either direction, only the road and the movement of rubber above it.

I'm alone in the same desert I left, in the world again and no longer *the Mind*. No longer the same strange shape resembling a metaphysical city.

And I know something about the sun now. I have an idea of where it's hidden. As the landscape rises through the climbing Arizona desert, up past Sedona and Flagstaff, into the crests surrounding Grand Canyon National Park, and then over the big coulee, that impressive gorge hurtling down into the core of the earth.

I have a sense of where the sun is missing. I know now where it's gone to hide. Wherever *M* is, the sun is not far behind. Wherever *M* is living, the sun is hidden in plain sight.

The landscape curves away from the catastrophes of

earth and reroutes towards the flatter terrain of the northern Arizona strip, then into Colorado City, Hildale, and soon the state of Arizona is far gone.

That leg of the drive is over. Hours removed from Tempe, and the topography transitions into a rocky and elevated version of before. A series of plateaus lining the horizon as an offering site to the firmament above, to that impressive dome on high.

No foot treads a mark on flat land, as Zion appears to the east—the rolling red preserve of jagged desert rockface, and rivers sunken emerald through sediment and dust. All layers of sand. Each one a marker of time and attrition, the impossibly slow passage of motion.

I know where the sun is. Just under the ridge of my slanted nose, it's there. Just beyond the frame of my farthest vision, it's hidden dimly, and hours north of where I am.

The bronze cliffs of Zion wrap northwardly bound through the ancient caverns of Angels Landing, where the broken rocks cast their shadows down the river to Sinawava, Paiute temple of the coyote god.

A coyote turns its eyes across the road. A flash of movement vanishes behind a massive boulder. Those concupiscent stones, each one rounder and more exaggerated than the last.

At turns, the landscape dictates the movement of the road around it. The highway meets the interstate again a dozen miles from Cedar City, from the address where *M* sent her letter, where I imagine her plane landed some time ago.

When I see her, I wonder if the memories that have gone missing will come surfacing back again, whether all of those years buried beneath a layer of sand will suddenly appear as I step through her door. What is this silence now? What is this giant cloud of unknowing? Is the truth in a world of blindness just that, unknowing? Is there any sense to hold on to in a landscape that filters through hands?

The sand dunes coarsen to rock in the side mirror of the baby blue toyota. What's left behind is no longer ahead. How did I end up in this car that I'd left behind, that I'd parked in the heart of *the Mind* outside a train station?

A track runs across the road, no train in sight. And *the Mind* makes less sense now than it did before. *Awoken with an egg on my head*, I think, and wonder whose mind I'd really been in, whether it was my own or somehow Dr. Higley's. As I look at my reflection in the mirror to my left, I see a face as clearly as day, two bright eyes and a downward-slanted nose, no smile, no posture, a patch of beard stretching coarsely over my skin.

I see myself again, again this stranger I've sensed for a month or more returned to me in a simple reflection. There again, I see the outline of an expression remarkably the same, an old inexpressible blankness, a note hollowed blue and soft in tone.

I'm crying before I can see myself. The tears fall before I know they're there. Returned again to the world anew, to the one I'd left some time ago, where my memory had taken me away.

H.A.

H.A., *H.A.*, my name, I remember, like a sudden shock of wind.

Like Dr. Higley's, *H.A.*, and yet different. And yet somehow I'm still not sure who Dr. Higley was, other than a strange parallel I met in throes of sleep. A hidden eye looking in.

As the highway winds ahead, a cedared peak appears and disappears through the depths of space. I adjust the radio as a familiar voice comes through it, the trembling baritone of Scott Walker, like a reminder of lost time. *Loneliness is the cloak you wear.* I tap on the gas as the road becomes more road. *A deep shade of blue is always there.* The highway becomes more highway. *The sun ain't gonna shine anymore. The moon ain't gonna rise in the sky. The tears are always clouding your eyes. When you're without love, baby.*

And soon the city limits of Cedar City approach, and a town coalesces at the foot of a large cedared mountain. A town where *M* is living. Where I've always imagined she's been in some way. As close to the foot of the sky as one could possibly be.

Who is *M* now, I wonder, but a dreamworld image?

Where has she gone, but the sky forever? Why go on searching for someone I can never see? I can only ever know in the faintness of dreams?

At the end of the highway, a road becomes a part of town. I park my car alongside it and step out, noticing a small regional airport, and across the way, a house numbered *7493*.

She's here, I think, and feel my heart collapse into my chest, into that cavern too splintered to feel most times.

Before I know it, I've walked across the driveway and I'm standing before her door. *The sun ain't gonna shine anymore.* And without knocking, without a movement at all, I notice the knob turn sideways, opening slowly, and she's there.

Northern star, oh eyesight.

M is standing there in the doorway, just as she is. No frame of memory, no filter of time. *M* is standing there as though no time has passed at all.

"Can I come in?" I ask.

M pauses, hesitates.

"Not right now," she says, *sorry*.

"That's okay," I say, standing in the doorway.

"I'm sorry," says *M*.

Her voice is just as it had sounded in my dreams. That same bright cadence that I'd remembered for so long.

"I think I know where the sun is," I mutter, without shifting my tone, but still *M* looks at me surprised, curious. "I think I know where the sun is hidden," I say, staring at *M* across the way.

Her face appears clearly, a moth just below her eyelash, the metal piercing above. As I stare longer, I can see *M* almost as I'd pictured, like a bright light too blinding to recall.

"I've been driving through a desert to get to you," I say. "I've been to Phoenix in my mind. I met a man named Dr. Higley in a town shaped like the sun. I've been sleeping with his egg on my head. I dreamed a city in the sky so I could see you, but the longer I've stared, the further I've drifted from the truth. *Which is that you're the sun, M. You're the one I've been looking for.*"

M stares at me, her eyes bright with an unclear meaning. As she stares, I hear a noise from the airport carry across space.

"Ever since you left, nothing has seemed to make sense. Nothing has mattered anymore. Because you were the center of the world, *M*. You're the one I've been missing."

M pauses without shifting her focus, her sightline directed straight and forward. As *M* stands in the doorway, I see time become an even more perplexing mystery.

"And I know, a month has seemed like a year has seemed longer, it's impossible to know the passage of time anymore. And I know I've been lost in a cross-wired mind, in confusion and thought. But I've been lost long before that, long before I ever met you, I lived in a world of confusion."

As I see *M* now, a feeling stirs from a hidden depth, an old memory flooding back from months of forgetting. As *M* stands before me, an old catastrophe casts its shadow across the doorway between us.

"When I was young, *M*, I lost someone who was important to me. It's funny, but standing before you now, I can remember it clearly."

As the airport quiets to a hum, as *M* stands in the passage of her doorway, a feeling comes rushing back. I see the faces of my parents long forgotten, like the faces of Dr. Higley and Martha Adic in Sun City, though not exactly the same.

"I remember my mother, when I was young, she lived with my father who was a doctor."

I see their faces in my mind's eye, the two of them as the couple I'd met in the desert town—identical names, though not exactly as I'd dreamed.

"When I was young, my mother, she left. She disappeared without warning."

○

"I was only a child then, so I don't remember much of it. Except that my father, he left too, but without leaving. When my mother left us, it was as though he entered a dream he couldn't wake from, as though I could never talk to him about any of it."

As I look at *M*, the past reveals an impossible shape.

"My father slept with an egg on his egg, so to speak, and that egg was me. I was his one unspoken hope, his chance at finding any peace in this world. But his vision of peace and mine were different. He dreamed of cities in the sky, but all I ever wanted was someone to talk to. And that was you, *M*. You were the light that showed myself to me. You showed me a love I never knew. And when you left, I fell back into that world without any light. Ever since you left, there's been no sun in the sky."

Across the road, the sound of a jet hurtles through space. It shoots across the runway and disappears into fading sound. As I see *M* now, her eyes fill with clouds of sorrow, of billowing shapes waiting to break the celestial plane. But as *M* stares at me longer, I can sense a dissonance pass just below the threshold of perception, a concern clouded beneath the surface of her gaze. As she begins speaking, I can almost guess each word as it comes out.

"I'm so sorry," she says, looking at me with a kindness I'd only forgotten, I'd only attributed to a past world. "I'm sorry, H.A., but I'm not the sun. I'm not the one who lives in your dreams."

A gut feeling freezes me still. I stand in the doorway motionless, watching *M* in the shadow cast by the light of her home. For a moment, as I look closer, I can see *M* appear not at all as I'd first thought. Her hair seems darker now. Her eyes sunken in the aperture of her face.

"I don't understand," I say, stuck in between two spaces, the one outside and in—a gut instinct catches me there with the sense of a truth I've known all along.

"*The sun is just gone,*" says *M*, staring at me through the doorway. "I'm sorry, H.A., but I'm not the one you've been looking for."

The sun is just gone.

I stare up at the sky now, at the wide expanse above the cedared peaks, and notice nothing's there—*the sky is entirely jet black.* The sky, as dark as night, appears clearly for the first time in as long as I can remember. No bright grey vision, no delusions of forever. The sky is simply black with night now.

How long has it been like this? I mutter, as *M* squints across the doorway, her torso cut in half by the stark shadow of light behind her, falling into the endless night outside.

"What's going on?" I say.

M looks at me now, a vision of worry crossing her face. She stands in the doorway as a stranger would, as an illusion of light.

"I know you," she says to me, in a voice that remains somehow steady and calm. "The two of us aren't so different," she says, gathering words which I've heard before and forgotten. "When I was young, I lost something too. Someone hurt me very badly. They didn't mean to, but they did. And like you, I moved through a world without the sun in it. I chased a light I never got to see. But the farther I chased it, the further it eluded me. The harder I tried to pin it down, the more easily it escaped. Because as much as I wanted to find it, I was only running away. I never stood in one place."

A wind passes through the doorway.

"When I met you, H.A., I saw a light I had never seen. I saw that thing I wanted so badly, which was to fly through the sky. Which was to be seen for who I was. And for a while, that's how things were. But as time went on, that old darkness crept back in. I began to feel like I was living a life that wasn't my own, that was a mere extension of your dream. Every waking moment I'd begun to feel like an image in your memory, like a role, *M*, that didn't belong to me. And as soon as I caught a glimpse of that, the sun went away. That light I'd seen when I met you disappeared."

○

"But for the longest time, you didn't notice. You went on dreaming this image of me, like a city in the sky that would last forever, but you didn't see me anymore. You saw this image you so desperately wanted me to be, this illusion of light I wasn't. I don't blame you anymore, but the longer you've stared at something that isn't there, the brighter it's become, the harder it is to see. The sun is just gone, H.A. It's just missing."

The bright grey delusions of the past fade into a stark reality of night, the sky simply without the sun in it. In my chest, I feel a wound fade as well, though I hold on as desperately as I can.

"But *M*," I say, seeing her across the doorway. "I'm not Dr. Higley. And I'm not Del Webb. I don't care about cities in the sky. I don't care about this vision you think I want you to be. I've been through the desert, and I know where the sun is now. I know where it is, *M*, if you'll just let me show you."

A noise from the airport breaks across space, a jet idling at the end of the runway. Its engine buzzes into the dark night invisibly, a noise cutting through the wind and sky.

For who knows how long, I've been lost in this bright confusion, this denial of reality whose truth I've danced around. I've been myself and someone else. I've been sleeping with an egg on my head. All of these roads I've driven, these leads I've followed, they've only led me further astray.

"It's not that I don't love you," says *M*, softly, as the wind dies down. "Because I do."

A jet makes a noise through the sky.

"It's just that the sun is gone. It's just gone."

I stand there in the doorway, as a second becomes a minute and an hour and longer. And without thinking about it, and without thinking at all, I head off into the night, into the dark sky as far as flying.

XX.
IT GOES

MY CAR FINDS its way back to Zion National Park.
To be honest, I don't know how I got here. The car must have driven on its own, because I don't remember ever pressing the pedal.

And I'm here, in a ravine near the Keyhole Canyon of eastern Zion. In a cleft where the northern crests and the southern crests meet at a singular point of conjunction. A narrow passage through the hardened impasses of earth.

And the sun is gone now, I see that. The sky a dark reality of missing light, of missing and missing. And that's all there is now. No blinding grey riddle pointing in any revelatory direction.

The world is a dark wilderness. And I feel all alone in this canyon dell, a pit in my throat and chest at all times sinking below me. And I've never felt so alone as I do now. In this wide-open space of the canyon which remains invisible to me.

For how long the sun has been missing, I don't know. For that man in the bar in Phoenix who said the sun had been missing his entire life, who said the sun had been missing as soon as the white settlers came to this part of the land, could it be missing that long?

My feet wend deeper into confusion and out, my car parked along the side of the road which I can't see anymore from this crevice of earth sneaking through the canyon walls. This stretch of time is a blur for me. This forgetting induced by a dream delusion, by a mirage fetched from the strangest depths of desert sand.

And now, nothing to be seen.

Do the same orders of power and domination, of sense and reason that the old sun presided over, do they carry on into this world, or are they gone now, like so much else that was once visible and now impossible to see?

Might a new order emerge from this? A paradigm of night over day, of those shadows once relegated to the other side of waking life, perhaps their world is at the center now?

Those creatures whose eyes adjust to the dim luminance of the moon, whose tongues click to form sight out of hearing, perhaps it's their world I've stepped into.

The canyon bends farther towards obscurity, winding into folded earth which remains entirely unseen. It is in moments like these that I begin to follow my thoughts more clearly, that the bright reflections of the waking day dim so that each form can carve its own outline.

An arrow pointed upward, slanted, a thought beside it turned around.

And I miss *M*, is the truth of it. Is the feeling turned round and matted in my throat. And I wonder if that's it, if I'll ever see *M* again on this earth spinning round. Or if she's just gone now, as missing as the sun is.

I reach out to feel the cleft walls turn softer, the hard Navajo sandstone becoming brittle and silted, and a dune shape emerges from them, which I climb up beneath the dark encasing of the sky.

The wind moves steady here, and I peer down at the narrow cleft behind, a faint line through larger darkness. My heart gasps at the thought of falling through it. How far a descent remains so unclear. My bones break at the thought of its basement.

I'd rather be there than here, in that old bright world than this one. Here I sense myself a kind of half-person, a centerless ghost ambling through the canyon walls without any sense of purpose or meaning. *M* was meaning, was that reflection of light that once showed myself to me, and without her, I'm not sure what point there is of moving on.

That old world moves farther away, and do I simply resign myself to that? To the gradual departure of this world that once held so much? Do I carry on with this purposeless crawl knowing that an old brightness was once here?

I'm lost again but my mind moves onward as my feet direct me, as I head back down the other end of the leeward slope.

Through miles of canyon, I notice a mesa vaguely rising in the distance. Miles before me, I see its outline cropping beneath the obsidian sky. And I wonder, maybe *M* isn't missing forever.

I wonder if, maybe, there's a new form of relation that's possible here. Not at the center, but around it. Not that old bright love, but a different kind. If somehow a shape can emerge in this nocturnal world that might present a new logic of relation.

A dry basin stretches for a mile, and I follow it straight towards the rising mesa in the distance. The arid soil beneath my feet makes a sound both the same and different, as time manages to move on despite the absence of days and nights. Despite the absence of color that used to suffuse each corner of stone.

What structures of power exist in this world? Is the domination of the sun no longer central? And if so, is that all there is of Sun City, is it returned to its resting place of sand?

I walk farther across the flat plane towards the mesa, the clouds above growing higher and denser than before, and somehow vision diminishes to an even bleaker form of shadow. The sounds of the canyon ricochet across walls miles apart, and in this falling blindness, I wonder if my senses will ever adjust? If my eyes might widen to take in more light, or my peripheral senses alter to replace what's lost now in vision? If olfaction and hearing might map themselves onto the spaces once occupied by sight?

Already I sense the sounds of the canyon more acutely. A drumming of cicadas in some brush somewhere, some thistle or shrub. A cricket maybe, a lunar beetle, each tuning their voices into the dark expanse of a nighttime sky.

Through the walls of a canyon like the walls of a house. No ceiling, no bed. No place to rest. And my feet draw farther towards the rising table of earth, the mesa which cuts sharply against an invisible backdrop.

I wonder how long I've been walking here. Could be a year, minutes, more or less? As time moves like the folded walls of the canyon dell—folded and patted through space, the same and different.

Who am I through it? What version of myself am I now, if anyone? What mirror is there here for me to see? Other than the pleats of dirt that crease beneath the weight of my ankles— my legs leaving no trail in this soil too arid to imprint.

I've been lost and lost again. Carved through the center. And soon I arrive at the base of the mesa whose shape I'd seen from some mileage away—the risen earth which now seems much taller than it had from afar.

If I wanted, I could imagine walking to the top of its flattened peak, several miles or so. But still my feet remain firmly planted onto soil, my neck arched back and head directed forward.

As I stare behind the mesa, I notice a thin line appear—a sharp band of blue sneaking just above the horizon stripe.

As I stare, I watch it bend and meet the outline of craters below, the canyon coming into view beneath its vague presence.

I see it there rising in the distance, a thin streak of silver or pink sneaking just above the canyon walls, as a letter dissolves itself through my chest, as I cling to the memory *M* as deeply as I can, I see a light sneak above the canyon ever so slightly.

But how?

And I realize now, as *M* shifts inside my feeling, holding on one last time, and seeing it there undeniably above the canyon rim.

Above the red canyon rim—the sun rising in the distance— a golden flame testing the morning air with its tepid light.

In the distance, I see it.

Oh god.

The sun rises, and I know *M* is gone.

EPILOGUE

XXI.
WAVING GOODBYE,
GOODBYE

HONEYCOMBS OF LIGHT spill in through the windows of the diner. Tempe, Arizona, again. I'm seated at a booth in the corner, a plate of eggs, bacon, potatoes and ketchup, toast, maple syrup, honey and jam. And the way the light comes in through the windows seems to circle each shape as if discovered for the first time, as if each object in the diner were surrounded with a sense of awakening.

I pull my coffee mug towards me and take a sip, as the sounds of the kitchen wash out over space and disperse there evenly, and leave the diner as quiet as the vague noises of plates and clatter.

And I've lived and died a thousand times in each breath. And I've lived and died a thousand times more.

I look up and see Tom again, and Pete again, the two of them seated at the counter just as they had been before. Tom crouched over a plate of eggs, a horseshoe mustache straddling his face. Pete a foot taller, his hair silken and buoyant in the falling light of the morning air.

Just then Pete gets up and walks over to the corner, puts a song on the jukebox and walks back. He asks Tom for a dance and the two of them amble towards the middle of the diner floor, as everyone around them seems to mind their own business, as the lines of light that peer through the windows reflect the entire space in a golden sheen.

Who's in love with that fantasy?
Who's in love with that image of me?

Pete grabs Tom at the waist and the two of them begin moving slowly back and forth, Pete leading as Tom follows, as Tom rests his head on Pete's shoulder and uses its weight as a cushion.

With an intuitive sensibility, Pete knows where to go without knowing, without seeing what's before him. He leads Tom in careful tracking movements, the two of them beginning slowly at the middle of the diner floor.

Breaking off, Pete rotates Tom's torso with a slow stroking orbit, clinging gently to the fabric of his shirt and then releasing with an invitation to follow. Tom feels the stretching pulse of denim through his shirtsleeve and watches as Pete moves beside him.

As Pete moves onward, he drifts in a series of gestures that resemble questions, his hands and arms posing to stop and accentuate each movement through space. *This? Why? How?* Tom cocks his head to the side and watches intently, as Pete punctuates each motion in turn.

Pete winks and the two suddenly break into a synchronized movement, bringing their arms over and back, leg kicked sideways swinging below, pas de bourrée and down. Pete spins loosely out of the movement, arms into the corner, accidentally swiping a silver napkin holder and sending it spinning in fractals of light around the room. Landing against a corner wall, Pete props his shoulders against it, arms spread up and down in a bilateral pose. He begins mouthing the lyrics of the song to Tom, who looks on bemused.

> *Who's in love with that mind projection?*
> *Who's in love with that illusion there?*
> *Who's in love with that only creation*
> *that projects into thin air?*

Pete's gaze fixes on Tom, whose eyes are closed now and hips swaying above the tile floor, as if standing on a floating saucer—Tom oils his knees and turns them slowly in rounds, gradually warming up his lower half. His movement is almost entirely internal, pacing, and Pete watches, stepping through patches of sunlight deflected through the window glass, his fingers moving with the bells of the rhythmic section, the strings on the back of his neck as he tiptoes towards the middle. Tom opens his eyes now and bends down to tie an undone shoelace, as Pete uses the opportunity to lunge over and employ Tom's knee as a staircase, launching himself briefly into the air, arms spread towards the sunlight of the east-facing glass. Pete turns back to Tom, who's fallen over into a puddle of ice, brushing himself off as Pete spins around and spreads his arms even further into the sunlight, leg behind him, swanlike, splitting the back of his jeans accidentally, and Tom laughs.

Standing upright, Tom turns and notices that Pete's fallen over as well, a single line of sweat running down his nose to the tile. Tom lunges away then returns to a rehearsed floor step, step step back, step step across support, step step back, step step across. Tom's movements are much more measured than Pete's, as if prearranged and repeated several times.

Pete gets up now and guilelessly returns towards Tom, who rolls Pete's body across the length of his arms and catches him on the other side in the crook of his elbow, holding Pete forty-five degrees above the ground.

And who's in love with the sky forever,

beyond, there's no never, everything can be?

Pete's shirt lifts above his waistline and a metal ring appears pierced at the center of his belly, scattering light across it and shining brightly in each cardinal direction. Tom lifts Pete from behind and rotates him horizontally to his feet, as the two of them resume a slow dance.

Pete whispers something and Tom responds back, the two of them clinging to each other closely. Their voices linger into mutters, *ahh, hmm,* then the movement of hands, Pete with his fingers just beneath Tom's shoulder blades, Tom sensing the chintz poplin fabric of Pete's bomber jacket. A whisper becomes the movement of an arm, Tom giving space for Pete to turn clockwise and back, Tom now leading their motion forward carefully, like a wary ship captain. Each step he takes ushers them further into uncharted waters, the light of the diner signaling a day both the same and entirely new. With each movement, Tom seems to shed a layer of concern, his motion becoming gradually more fluid.

The two of them sway in place awhile, now standing on the same floating saucer, as if now tossing and turning over the course of the same night's sleep. Each motion bestows an unconscious process, a movement eliciting a feeling the two of them are working through without their knowledge, a turn to the left creating one sort of feeling, a toss forward creating another. Tom mutters a word that transmutes into sound, into the feeling of the ground below his feet, Pete meeting him there and whispering something back. "Have you heard this song before?" "Did *Anna Lee* say anything?" The light from the windows shimmers from Tom's eyes over to Pete and back again, as the two of them sway in place for a minute longer, then wake up from a trance.

Who's in love with this vision of peace?
Who's in love with possibilities?

At a certain point, Pete retreats to the counter to remove his blue glossy bomber, its chintz fabric picking up the heat of the morning air. He slides his arm out of the left sleeve, as if still dancing and yet perfectly natural, then slouching to his right and pulling the rest over top of his head, leaving his silken hair standing upright and static. He throws the vest over the back of his chair and turns around, then notices me watching from my booth in the corner, the only one in the diner who seems to be paying any attention at all.

For a moment he simply stares with his hair upright, then begins heading towards me, the sound of his sneakers on the ground overriding the pace of music, step step, still dancing and yet walking perfectly natural over to my table, staring down at me, then dipping his fingers into my water glass and pressing his hair down with it, flattening the top of his head again and returning his wet hand towards me with an invitation to follow, to get up from my seat and move.

I stare at Pete and he stares back, his face tomato red from the heat of his movement, his eyes impatient and waiting. I stare up unable to alter, paralyzed by some unknowable force keeping my feet planted on the ground. Pete lingers for what seems unexpectedly long, then turns around to head back towards Tom and in that moment, I get up to follow him, and move towards the middle of the diner, finding my feet one by one below me.

Who's in love with the one and only?

Pete tugs Tom's sleeve and spins him towards me—Tom's arms nudge mine, sending me loosely into my body, my joints calibrated to the weight of his impact. I feel my neck carry a pulse all the way to the floor, my hips responding by creasing back and bending my upper half forward, diagonal with the ground, then my toes leaving as well, and swiveling on the heels of my feet.

No one in the diner seems to notice our motion, a trio of forms spinning in place. I see Tom and Pete as well, each body in its own frame of reference, carving a non-Euclidian geometry through space.

Who's in love with this divine image?

My head meanwhile grows heavy and rolls two full ovals round, then my shoulders tensing to my ears and releasing through the ends of hands, eyelids closed but still sensing the warmth on the other side of them, the diner aglow in a new sort of heat.

Who's in love with it now, this way?

Pete hooks elbows with mine and gleefully places his arms beside me, using my support as a means to leave his balance for a moment and then catch it again, and then turn on a slanted axis towards Tom, who awaits his fall. Tom nods a note of reassurance towards me, and I return to my movement from before, my neck feeling a cord with the ground, carrying me above it both abandoned and connected.

My instinct takes me halfway across the floor, the thudding of my feet shaking the plates and glasses on the tables surrounding, my focus entirely spread across each end of the diner. With eyes wide open, I find myself caught in the light of the room, entangled in the invisible field of energy moving between each object in space. I fall into it, my body easing into the sense of edges, places to be held and pushed away, the momentous force of movement spinning from one motion to the next.

Inside a deep cavity, a surge of light shoots through my chest and opens a window into somewhere else. It slaps me into tears, awake from a dream, an unconscious process into a moment of realization.

My arm waves beside me, and I carry my weight below it, following its uncertain path around. Has this dream been just that, an act of forgetting? Moving far enough away to let something in? I sense it rising somewhere within me and carrying another motion forward. I wave my arm.

Across the diner floor, I notice Tom and Pete there still, Pete watching Tom as he prepares a motion across the length of the diner.

I stand and watch as well, as Tom eyes the space before him, as he prepares a motion it seems he must have practiced for months. Pete's movements are reduced to a steady onlook, mine as well, as Tom takes a final breath and runs lunging into the air before him, eyes set on a spot across the diner floor, leaping towards it, arms spread, knees bent and toes pointed downward, balletic, virtuosic, Tom leaping across the length of the diner without regard for anything besides himself, soaring, floating a foot above the ground and racing there, suspended—he turns his heels and begins a rotation, once, twice around, elegantly, a double axel, then turns his focus again to the spot right before him, as if reborn, his shadow following behind in the falling light, and I sense it too, the movement from one space to another, from one world to the next, Tom now descending slowly to the other side of the diner, brightly through the light, a yard or so from where he leapt, his knees straightening so that his legs can meet the ground, right foot first, left following, gracefully landing and bowing with the momentum of his force, catching him on the other side, and the music cuts out.

> *Who's in love with that dreamworld image*
> *that only begot in fantasy?*

Tom lands and stands on the other end of the diner, as the noises disperse for a moment, as Pete and I look on from our respective corners in wonder, then I watch as Tom walks back to the counter, and Pete follows, the two of them sitting down as the waitress comes over to refill their glasses.

I watch her lift a pitcher, then head towards a booth and fill a glass there. On her pinafore I notice a name tag reading *Anna Lee* across the front—then she walks past me to the counter again and lays her name tag facedown above it. She removes her pinafore and heads out the doors into the parking lot. I watch as she walks halfway across to her car, pulling out a pack of cigarettes and smoking one into the air before getting in. She stands there awhile, and I watch through the window as she reaches again for her pocket and pulls out a key.

○

Anna Lee gets in the car and starts driving. She heads onto the highway and goes a mile, another mile, an exit, another exit, onto a road which turns into a town at the edge of the desert.

She drives down a lane, turns left, drives down another, then goes straight. At the end of a stretch a man appears outside his driveway watering an oakleaf hydrangea. Anna Lee pulls over the car next to him and parks it, leaving the engine on.

Rick, she says, and the man comes over, putting down his hose. He asks Anna Lee if she's just gotten off work—she nods yes, that she won't have work again until the evening— Rick says something dry, then a woman comes out of the house behind him and gets in the car with Anna Lee.

They drive some more, onto the highway again, farther into the desert until it becomes a turnoff, the entrance to a state park. Anna Lee pulls over and leaves her sedan beneath some shade. She and her friend step out, then head onto a trail.

Anna Lee and her friend could be sisters, though Anna Lee's friend is many years younger, could even be her daughter. The two of them have the same dark curly hair, sequin eyes, a way of saying words as though leaving them hanging, as though discarding thoughts as soon as they're said.

"I think there's a lake here," says Anna Lee, heading up a sloping trail. Her friend follows just behind her, bending down to grab a bit of sage which she passes to Anna Lee who smells it and says something pleasant.

"You know, the last time I was here, I think it rained, which is very uncommon."

Eventually the trail levels out and the two of them see a lake appear in the distance, a clear reflection of the sky approaching closer, and Anna Lee and her friend sit beside it, dipping their hands into the water.

Anna Lee's friend pulls out a cigarette and smokes it, and Anna Lee grabs something from her bag to eat, a candy bar which she unwraps.

"My mom sold the house," says Anna Lee's friend, holding the cigarette beside her. She speaks carelessly, tossing her words into the air with a tone of detachment. Anna Lee doesn't know exactly how to respond so she remains in a distant state herself, letting her friend's words slowly move across the length of the lake.

Its surface shifts as the sun moves above it, as the clouds alter the intensity of light. The day becomes the movement of the clouds above them, and the sun slowly keeping score.

Anna Lee returns the wrapper to her bag and leans back

slightly, finding a rock to rest her head on. Her friend stays staring at the surface of the water, watching it maintain itself in place.

"Sometimes I think of myself as a color," says Anna Lee, staring up at the sky, watching it stay still for a moment longer. "And when I think of myself as a color, it helps me forget how I usually think of myself. And I used to think of myself as red, but recently I've been thinking of myself as yellow."

Anna Lee's friend outs the cigarette and tosses it onto the ground. She lies back too and rests her head so that she can still see the water's surface.

No life moves as far as she can tell. No signs of fish or birds, the occasional insect but otherwise a strange desert quietness. A few junipers make a noise behind them, but no other trees appear around.

In this part of Arizona, the air is as dry as any desert but the elevation produces a chilling effect. The air is not quite as hot as it would be around Phoenix or Tempe, and as a result, Anna Lee pulls a sweater from her bag and drapes it around her. Her friend, also cold, tucks her hands into her sleeves.

As the sun curves onward, it moves behind some clouds, and the sky reflects a change in the lake below it.

"Holding on is what hurts," says Anna Lee's friend, looking out at the lake as it becomes a new shadow. "I think that's the source of the pain."

Light breaks through a cloud past the lake on the other side of it, a mile or so.

"But I loved that house," says Anna Lee's friend, looking across the water. "I don't want to forget it."

An hour goes by and the two of them move on to another topic, to a long stretch of silence that doesn't feel uncomfortable to either of them. In fact, they hardly notice how quiet it is at all, the lake as still as a windless day.

Anna Lee smokes a cigarette herself and her friend watches a group of four pass along the trail and leave shortly after. The two of them are alone at the lake, except for a man way in the distance with a fishing pole in the water.

"This lake reminds me of a lake I would go to when I was living in Poland," says Anna Lee, staring out from the rock. "And I would go there with my brother when we were little, and we wouldn't swim in the water because it was mostly marsh, but we'd walk alongside it and watch the fish."

The sun moves to a three-quarters position, and the sky

deepens with the encroachment of night. As Anna Lee stares out, her friend looks over at her, studying her the same way she'd studied the lake, with a curious distance.

"Did I ever meet your brother?" she asks, and Anna Lee shakes her head no.

"That was someone else," she says.

Soon the lone fisherman across the lake reels in his line for the day, taking his gear and cooler with him on the trail. Anna Lee doesn't notice until he's gone, then stares across the lake and sees it deepen with the sky.

"Are you working this evening?" she asks, and her friend nods yes. "I am as well," says Anna Lee, grabbing a few of her things.

Before the sun moves any further, the two of them pack up and head back onto the desert trail, following their steps towards the car in the waning light. Anna Lee pulls another cigarette from her pocket and smokes it into the air, as evening descends upon the two of them suddenly.

Their story is just one among many stories under the same ever-changing sky, under the same impossible constellation of stars as always.

Anna Lee climbs in the car and opens the passenger's door. She adjusts her side mirrors, looks in the rear, then stares over at her friend. "Are we forgetting anything?" she asks, and hits the gas, and sends the car flying into the night.

APPENDIX

I. MEDULLA OBLONGATA

Oldest region of the central nervous system, and most anterior, *Medulla Oblongata*, slanted middle, forms the transition from spinal cord to brain. It is integral to some of the most basic functions of the central nervous system, coughing, vomiting, sneezing, and other involuntary, reflexive acts. It is most chiefly responsible for the regulation of cardiovascular and respiratory function, signaling to the diaphragm when to expand and contract breath. All of the *Medulla Oblongata*'s function occurs at an autonomic level, regulating the body's function without the conscious mind's awareness.

II. THALAMUS

Located just above the *Medulla* and brain stem, the *Thalamus* serves as a relay station, a midpoint of information among distinct and often distant regions of the brain. It relays information from sensory receptors, visual, auditory, to conscious regions of perception and processing. It is also responsible for relaying information related to motor function as well as other processes such as memory, emotional regulation, and sleep. The *Thalamus* is one of the busiest, most connected regions of the brain, constantly bridging information from conscious, unconscious, and semiconscious regions of the nervous system.

III. CORPUS CALLOSUM

A nerve tract of white matter that runs across the midline of the brain, connecting the left and right hemispheres, and allowing for communication between them. The brain is segmented into two nearly identical halves, separated along the *Medial Longitudinal Fissure*, and each half receives distinct sensory information from the body's external organs. The *Corpus Callosum* allows for an exchange of information between the halves, providing a singular, unified experience of consciousness. Each half, or cerebral hemisphere, is a near mirror of the other, with marked differences in processing, the left hemisphere more responsible for linear forms of cognition, while the right more often correlated to associative thought.

IV. CAUDATE NUCLEUS

This bundle of nerves within the subcortical structure *Basal Ganglia* is implicated in the regulation of motor function. Situated astride the *Thalamus*, it integrates spatial information with movement, keeping track of spatial working memory while orchestrating the body's motion through it. As well as motion, *Caudate Nucleus* is involved in a variety of disparate cognitive functions such as sleep, memory and learning, desire, and language. Like all regions of the brain, it works in concert with its surrounding, as well as distant, neuroanatomical neighbors, to integrate spatial memory with other forms of memory and cognitive function. In this way, like all areas of the brain, it performs its specific function through connection to larger neural networks, constantly changing and adapting to a fluid system.

V. SUBSTANTIA NIGRA

This black substance within the brain, which gets its color from large expressions of neuromelanin pigment, is directly involved in the regulation and facilitation of movement. Like *Caudate Nucleus*, it is a subcomponent of *Basal Ganglia*, and is split into two segments known as *Pars Compacta* and *Pars Reticulata*. *Pars Compacta*, comprised heavily of dopamine neurons, which contain large expressions of neuromelanin, communicates directly with the rest of *Basal Ganglia* to orchestrate smooth, controlled motor function. For individuals with Parkinson's disease, this region of the brain often finds itself depleted of dopamine-receiving neurons, resulting in the disregulation and breakdown of fine motor function.

VI. HIPPOCAMPUS

A seahorse-shaped structure of the brain, *Hippocampus* is responsible primarily for the formation and consolidation of short-term and long-term memory. Memory formation occurs through a process known as long-term potentiation (LTP), which is the strengthening and weakening of connections among nerve endings between distinct regions of the brain. The continued strengthening or weakening of these connections creates a network of association that becomes the constituents of memory. The stronger and more repetitively these connections are reinforced by various stimuli, the more consolidated a particular memory may become. When these associations and correlations are not repeatedly reinforced, the memories they constitute become weaker and less immediate, resulting in the process of forgetting. In individuals who have suffered brain trauma of some kind, a blunt injury to the head, a serious tumor or hemorrhage, connections among distinct regions of the brain find themselves physically ruptured and divided, and the networks of association that constitute a given memory can dramatically fissure, resulting in sudden memory loss and forgetting.

VII. WERNICKE'S AREA

Named after the German physician Carl Wernicke, who studied the region in the late nineteenth century, this area of the left cerebral hemisphere is involved in the comprehension of language. Wernicke reported that patients with damage to this region experienced deficits in understanding the semantic and linguistic sense of words. Individuals with what has become known as *Wernicke's Aphasia* would produce speech that resembled fluent language but was in fact meaningless, comprised of nonsensical, sometimes completely made-up words, or words that sounded similar to other words and substituted in their place (paraphasias). He presented a model involving the nearby *Broca's Region* to explain how semantic meaning was produced in the brain. *Broca's Region*, which is involved in the *production* of speech, tongue movement, syntax, grammar, verbal memory, would interact with *Wernicke's Area* to produce coherent language. Individuals with damage to *Broca's Region* would exhibit the ability to *understand* speech, but not *produce* it. Conversely, individuals with *Wernicke's Aphasia* could *produce* speech but not in any coherent form. With this model, Wernicke developed a concept of speech comprehension in the brain that involved a dual relationship between these two regions, *Broca's* responsible for the production of speech and *Wernicke's* for language comprehension. Now many believe that this model of linguistic formation in the brain is a simplistic one, and that in fact numerous regions of the central nervous system are implicated in the complex mechanics of language; however, it is clear that *Wernicke's Area* is directly implicated in the most fundamental aspects of language production.

VIII. AMYGDALA

Part of the *Limbic System*, this almond-shaped cluster is involved in the integration of emotional memory. In connection with *Hippocampus*, as well as other arms of the *Limbic System,* it is responsible for triggering the body's physical reaction to an emotional stimulus. For example, certain conditioned fear responses find their activation through *Amygdala*, whereby a specific stimulus may trigger the body's fight-or-flight response to a situation. In individuals with post-traumatic stress disorder, even nonthreatening stimuli can trigger a fight-or-flight response in the body, as *Amygdala* associates these stimuli with a given traumatic event. The *Amygdala* is directly implicated in sexual arousal and desire, experiences of negative valence and positive valence emotion, aggression, fear, as well as emotional modulation and consolidation of memory. In a 1994 study of a woman referred to as *S.M.*, who'd had her *Amygdala* completely destroyed from a childhood disease, researchers observed that the subject displayed no fear response to stimuli. Researchers took S.M. to haunted houses, snake stores, horror films, but observed no fear of any of these predictably scary scenarios, elucidating to them the likely role of *Amygdala* in fear response. Additionally, individuals may experience *Capgras Delusion*, which is an extremely rare psychiatric disorder brought on from a variety of sources, traumatic brain injury, neurodegeneration, paranoid schizophrenia; it displays its effect with a delusion in which stimulus that once held deep emotional significance—the face of a loved one, a parent, a friend—can appear exactly as it had before but stripped of its emotional valence, causing the individual to suspect that whoever they are seeing is an identical imposter. An fMRI study conducted in 1998 by V. S. Ramachandran determined that the likely cause of such delusions is the dramatic fissuring of connections between the visual regions of the brain and the emotional *Amygdala*, causing one to experience vision intact, and emotion intact, but severed from one another, resulting in the uncanny effect of an imposter image. A similar and related syndrome, *Cotard Delusion*, involves the same neural pathways, in which individuals experience themselves and everything around them as *dead*, lacking the emotional resonance of life and therefore subsumed into a dead world.

IX. SOLAR PLEXUS

A radiating cluster of nerves located just before the aorta, *Solar Plexus* marks the center of the peripheral nervous system, which is the segment of the nervous system that lies outside of the brain and spinal cord. It is categorized into two distinct systems, *somatic* and *autonomic*, which distinguish themselves based on the type of movement they innervate. In *somatic innervations*, movement is voluntary, signaled consciously from the brain to the body. *Autonomic innervations* occur without the conscious brain's input, often eliciting reflexive movements of the body, as well as regulating internal organs. In the case of *Solar Plexus*, the gut is the primary internal organ of contact, sending its biochemical information to the brain and receiving information back, a reciprocal exchange that keeps the central nervous system and the body in constant communication, dispelling any misconception that thought is located solely within the confines of the skull.

X. OPTIC CORTEX

Located in the *Occipital Lobe*, the *Optic Cortex* is the center of visual processing. It is here that light information from the eyes, refracted through the lenses, absorbed by the pupil, received onto the surface of photoreceptors, transduced by proteins beneath the *Retina*, signaled along nerve fibers, crossing at the *Optic Chiasm*, passing the *Lateral Geniculate Nucleus*, reaches the point of visual cognition. It is here that the chaos of light and darkness finds its coherence through the consolidation of recognizable patterns and shapes. The *Optic Cortex* does this by organizing *columns*, which are the linear constituents of light. These columns are grouped together to form two-dimensional images, which are then given an additional dimension through binocular depth perception—a product of the left and right eyes' distinct visual fields. The *Optic Cortex* is also responsible for synthesizing color information, which is received as *blobs*, units of color input organized in a cylindrical manner and then unified into one recognizable color. This color information is received through two types of photoreceptors on the *Retina*, those that innervate blue/yellow light, *K-cells*, and those that innervate red/green light, *P-cells*. These cells send their information along specific nerve fibers to the *Optic Cortex*, where color, depending on frequency and brightness, combine red/green information with blue/yellow to form all conceivable colors of human sight. These colors map themselves onto the columns and borders of light/dark information to form the constituents of an image. It is significant to note that all images that arrive to the *Optic Cortex* arrive first as reversed images, flipped upside down across the vertical axis. This is a product of the eye's outer lens, which reverses the projection of light as it enters the pupil. Only in the *Optic Cortex* does this reversal correct itself, flipping images right side up again. Similarly, when light enters the visual field, there is always necessarily a spot missing at the center of sight, a *scotoma*, which results from the *Optic Disc* at the center of the *Retina*, where no light reception occurs. Only in the *Optic Cortex* does this blind spot, *punctum caecum*, find correction, smoothing over the missing point at the center of sight to create the illusion of a continuous visual field.

XI. OPTIC NERVE

On the surface of the *Retina*, there are two primary forms of light receptors, *rods* and *cones*. The *rods* exist at the periphery of the eye, and they collect light/dark information. *Cones* reside closer to the middle, along the *fovea*, and they collect information on color, blue/yellow from *K-Cells*, and red/green from *P-Cells*. The *rods* and *cones* send their information to the *Optic Cortex* via the *Optic Nerves*, one extending from the right eye, and the other from the left. The *Optic Nerves* are essentially optic cables carrying electric charges of light and color information to the central nervous system. The cables, or nerve tracts, which are insulated by myelin sheath to ensure the rapid movement of charge, can be subdivided into five primary fibers, V1–V5. V1 is a sorting area, a nerve tract that passes information along to the more complex fibers of V2–V5. V2 is responsible primarily for figure representation, passing light information that is relevant to the shapes and borders of images in space. V3, also known as the "what/where" pathway, is responsible for the location of objects in space, both "where" they are and "what" they are. The "where" pathway moves along the dorsal side of V3, while the "what" pathway moves along the ventral side, passing information to the V4 fiber, which carries color data to the brain. The "where" pathway transitions to V5, which carries motion information, the movement of objects through space. The *Optic Nerves*, which carry light from the left eye and right eye respectively, decussate at the *Optic Chiasm*, moving information from the left visual field to the right brain, and right to left. They pass through the *Lateral Geniculate Nucleus*, before arriving at the *Optic Cortex*.

XII. SUPERIOR COLLICULUS

Connected to the *Lateral Geniculate Nucleus, Superior Colliculus* is responsible primarily for the maintenance of eye saccades: the rapid and unconscious movement of eyes to adjust their point of fixation, allowing one to walk around and move one's head without having to worry about one's visual field moving as well. The *Superior Colliculus*, which works unconsciously, regulates the body's reaction to external stimuli at large, adjusting not just eye saccades but arm reaches, head turns, and the body's overall unconscious orientation to visual stimuli in space.

XIII. CUNEUS

A wedge-shaped lobe within the *Occipital Lobe* of the brain, *Cuneus* is involved in basic visual processing. It is situated above the *Calcarine Sulcus*, and like all visual areas of the brain, it resides at the very back of the skull, rostral and superior to the *Medulla* and brain stem. Its specific functions include basic processing of vision at the bottom of the visual field, as well as connecting visual regions surrounding it, the *Optic Cortex* and neighboring structures.

XIV. OPTIC RADIATION

A set of nerve tracts that transmit visual information from the *Lateral Geniculate Nucleus* to the *Optic Cortex*, its structure can be segmented into the *upper division* and *lower division*. If a lesion occurs in the *upper division*, which includes structures such as *Meyer's Loop*, a phenomenon known as "pie in the sky" can occur, in which the upper quadrants of sight become blind. Similarly, if a lesion occurs in the *lower division*, "pie in the floor" transpires, a blind spot at the bottom of sight.

XV. OPTIC CHIASM

After the Latin *Chi*, meaning *X*, the point at which the two *Optic Nerves*, left and right, decussate across the midline. The left visual field crossing towards the right cerebral hemisphere, and right to left conversely. Without information from both eyes, images would appear in two dimensions, lacking the depth provided by a distinct vantage only two points of reference can confer. Creatures such as fish, horses, lizards, and many others, whose eyes reside on opposite sides of their face, see the world as two images, one on the left, one on the right, each as two-dimensional renderings of space. Those with blindness in one eye, or who simply shut an eyelid closed, will notice that depth is still perceived despite the lack of binocular disparity. This is due, in effect, to the brain's ability to detect depth in the absence of dual vision, using cues such as relative size of objects, motion of objects through space, the curved nature of peripheral vision, and other visual signs that allow a rough sense of depth in the absence of stereoscopic vision.

XVI. SUPRACHIASMATIC NUCLEUS

There are three forms of light receptors on the inner surface of the eye: the *rods*, which detect light/dark information, the *cones*, which detect color information, and the *intrinsically photosensitive*, which detect light that travels to unconscious regions of the brain. Among these regions include the *Pretectum*, which controls pupillary light reflex, the *Superior Colliculus*, which controls eye saccades, and the *Suprachiasmatic Nucleus*, an unconscious region of the visual system responsible for regulating the brain's circadian clock.

This small nucleus, located just above the *Optic Chiasm*, within the bounds of the *Hypothalamus*, receives light information that orients the brain within a twenty-four-hour cycle, detecting the movement of sunlight over the course of the day to regulate the brain and body's diurnal patterns: sleeping, waking, eating, hormonal release.

In the absence of light, or in the presence of excessive light, individuals may experience something known as *circadian dysrhythmia*, in which the function of the *Suprachiasmatic Nucleus* is obscured as a result of shifting light exposure, causing an aberrant firing of hormone release, disrupting sleep and wake cycles, as well as other metabolic patterns.

In addition to human eyesight, a version of the *Suprachiasmatic Nucleus* exists in most creatures, including even insects, bees, ants, planthoppers, flies. In bees, this nucleus serves as a sort of celestial compass, orienting a bee's understanding of space in relation to the location of the sun. Because of sunlight's electromagnetic properties, bees can determine the sun's location based on the angle of its ultraviolet rays. A bee detects this angle with a special sort of photoreceptor on its eye that is sensitive to the directionality of UV light, comparing that information to its internal clock, to form a coordinate understanding of space. If the sun is at a certain position in the sky, at a certain hour of the day, a bee knows exactly where it is located. This allows bees to remember the location of their hive and the location of pollinating flowers at great distances. It also provides the mechanism by which they perform what is known as their *waggle dance*, a figure-eight movement that conveys information to other bees about the location of flowers in the area. The duration and movement of this dance signals to other bees exactly where they can find flowers using their shared coordinate understanding. Interestingly, in a sort of parallel evolution, many flowers reflect ultraviolet light, signaling their location to bees using a similar optic mechanism.

Dung beetles, like bees, possess a similar celestial compass, though theirs are attuned to the electromagnetic rays of moonlight. Nocturnal dung beetles, unlike diurnal, have large light receptors on their eyes that allow them to magnify light in dark conditions. This magnification, which allows for their attunement to the location of the moon, provides a coordinate understanding of space. It is why dung beetles are able to travel great distances at night through deserts, moving their dung balls in a straight line without losing track of their location.

Similarly, humans—though diurnal creatures—have mechanisms for sensitizing eyesight at night. Compared to certain nocturnal life-forms such as owls or raccoons, whose eyes are specifically oriented to darkness, humans have a significantly more difficult time seeing at night. Still, the human visual system employs an array of techniques for increasing sensitivity to light, including temporal summation, in which light signals are consolidated over longer periods of time, resulting in increased brightness, but overall lag and blurriness. Another method the eye employs is spatial summation, in which multiple light receptors group their information together to increase light sensitivity, resulting in the ability to see more at night but with decreased resolution. This is why vision at night becomes not just dimmer but less exact.

The *Suprachiasmatic Nucleus*, as one of the oldest and most basic parts of the human visual system, and found in almost all creatures, points to a fundamental connection between the function of sight and the nervous system's relation to celestial cycles, the movement of the sun over the course of the day, and the body's orientation to it.

Even for individuals who are blind, the *Suprachiasmatic Nucleus* is still able to receive unconscious light information—so long as the eye structure is intact—orienting the brain to a twenty-four-hour light cycle despite the absence of any conscious light awareness.

This signals something substantial about the function of the brain, which is that the vast majority of its cognitive function occurs at an unconscious level. Almost all of the nervous system's wiring falls outside the realm of conscious awareness, operating in a space almost entirely inaccessible to deliberate thought. The small portion of the brain's wiring that is deliberate, *conscious awareness*, is itself a form of clouded mystery, an eye at the center of an unconscious system. Maurice

Merleau Ponty, a twentieth-century French phenomenologist, regarded the mystery of consciousness, of the *eye/I*, as a point that, despite seeing that which surrounds it, is incapable of seeing itself. That the point from which one looks is a point that can never be seen, that remains invisible, by virtue of its own properties.

ACKNOWLEDGMENTS

For emi kuriyama, rabbit over the moon, without whom I'd never have learned to write, for nissa sage gustafson, robert merritt, fernanda sanchez luna, avery raimondo, helena deland-mccullagh, liz ayre, the incredible jon wagner, thank you, for the incommensurate mentorship of jonathan lethem, for effy morris, charlie bond, elicia epstein, hayley parry, maggie nelson for being supportive every step of the way, the blue house, esplanade, morgan parker, for my sister liora, for my parents sharon and brad, and for ma.

Everyone at Melville House, Dennis Johnson, Valerie Merians, Mike Lindgren, Beste M. Doğan, Sofia Demopolos, Janet Joy Wilson, Sammi Sontag, Ariel Palmer-Collins, thank you to Laura Jeffery for choreographing Tom and Pete's dance in the final chapter, and thank you of course to the one and only, almighty, god.